THE W.H.I.F.F. FACTOR

by

JOHN WOOD

WOLFHOUND PRESS

First published 1994 by
WOLFHOUND PRESS Ltd
68 Mountjoy Square
Dublin 1

and Wolfhound Press (UK)
18 Coleswood Road, Harpenden
Herts AL5 1EQ

Wolfhound Press receives financial assistance from the Arts Council / An Chomhairle Ealaíon, Dublin, Ireland

This book is fiction. All characters, incidents and names have no connection with any persons living or dead. Any apparent resemblance is purely coincidental.

British Library Cataloguing in Publication Data

Wood, John
  W.H.I.F.F.
  I. Title
  823.914 [J]

  ISBN 0-86327-400-5

Cover illustration: Aileen Caffrey
Typesetting: Wolfhound Press
Printed by the Guernsey Press Co Ltd, Guernsey, Channel Isles

1

The Sunday Sermon

By the age of twelve she had seen it all; that's how it felt to Audrey: the changes, the despair on people's faces, global warming, the end of fossil fuel.

Life as they had known it, had changed. And the heat and the rain! And now the sweat was streaming off her elfin-like face, soaking her pale gold hair, as she waited in St Michael's for the service to begin. Her uncle Bernie sometimes called her Angel, except she didn't feel like one: changing her dress often twice a day ... just a quick rinse through, and then trying to dry it in the humid air. It often made her angry, the way things were: what had happened.

All around it was hot. In the distance, from off the fields, the heat and moisture rose in great plumes into the bright, hanging mists.

The doors of St Michael's had been left open for the breeze that slid across the town and over the shining roofs. All the same it was hot in the church, too.

~

It was hot like it used to be also in the pizza parlour on a Friday night.

Pizza-making, television, night-time football under the arc-lights; all that sort of thing had finished with the end of power, although electricity came on for one or two hours in the mornings, weekdays only, not on Sundays. That was for cooking; also for television, which was, more often than not, to do with government announcements: they were so boring! It was not lawful to use machines to make anything. Nothing was made any more except food, and that was mainly at home. Places like pizza-parlours could not stay in business, opening just two hours a day. All the McDonald's had closed.

Because of the global warming, because it was so hot and damp, plants grew madly. Things that took only the sun energy were fine. Pigs still grunted. Blackberries ripened.

Because of the end of fossil fuel, people used candles now. In this respect it was like a hundred or more years ago. You talked at night because there was no television, and people looked younger and softer; their noses, foreheads, and lips glistening in the candle-light. Every Sunday the church glowed with candles. There were enough candles locked away in the crypt to last for another year at least, by which time the hopeful ones thought the new-age power would be in place.

It had all started with the melt-downs, she remembered; one after the other it had seemed; even the sheep glimmering at night with radioactivity. This had started the clamour, the panic worldwide to shut down the nuclear reactors. Which they had done!

By then, even the oil had run low; of course everyone had known it would. Most of the coal mines were now closed; many flooded or producing gas to drive the turbines. But the ways that were left, including solar panels and wind power, were not enough for the grid. So the power came on for two hours; long enough to cook a meal weekdays.

Meanwhile on television, people were urged to put up with it a little longer: with the two hours; to hold on! Worldwide they were ready to build the atomic fusion plants, but still the point of ignition had not been reached. Here, scientists were using power generated from the remains of the North Sea gas to make plasma ten times hotter than the sun. Once the plasma could produce enough power for itself, it would form the core of a nuclear reactor. All this was explained on television, Audrey understanding it all, only too well, although people like Mr Hood who kept pigs down the Ossington Road, out of town, could not take it in, and would often just use the time when the power was on to fry up some sausages.

It was going to be a miracle for humankind, a source of limitless power, they said, for the millions who now waited and sweated. And in the meantime this small part of humankind, the hundred or so in the congregation of St Michael's was fidgeting in the heat! There was no escape.

~

Audrey Oliphant fidgeted too as she sat with her
parents in the family pew. Her father, Major Oliphant,
held himself severely and bent down from time to time
to say something to his wife, Priscilla, a delicate lady in
blue. He felt at home in St Michael's, among the
Oliphants of stone and marble; ancestral figures set into
the wall along one side of the church, where they were
warmed at certain times by the sunlight glowing with
colours from the stained glass windows.

At last the bell-tower door opened and the procession
moved down the aisle. As it passed the Oliphants,
Audrey whispered, 'Just look at his feet!'

These days of course everybody was ready for anything, for the things people did: their outrageous mood
changes; their anger at the way things were; their
anxiety as they tried to manage. But for all that, the
congregation did not expect to see the vicar come down
the aisle in his bare feet, although they understood the
causes well enough.

It was because of the wretched dampness, the ever-
lasting rain, always the rain, in between the hot sun and
the low mists that filled the ditches, and which so often
ended in the misery of wet socks.

How much everybody longed for wellingtons! But
of course, with no oil and none of the plastics which
were made from it, there were no wellingtons to be had.
They were all in the same situation, except for Audrey
and her parents, and her friend Oliver of course, and his
family. They all had them.

The Major did not know how many he had in store:
over a thousand pairs anyway, all safely locked up.
Now as he listened to the sermon, his irritation was

obviously increasing. Whenever people spoke to him of feet, he felt as if they were asking him for wellingtons.

'And people have been so kind to me.' the vicar was saying, talking of his journeys by foot to visit the sick. 'One dear lady insisted on drying my socks, which alas, as you will have guessed, have become wet again ...'

'It's a cheek,' Major Oliphant whispered.

'Keep calm, Dad,' Audrey breathed. Without moving her head too noticeably, she looked at some of the congregation. Many had worked in his wellington factory, in the Oliphant Footwear Co, and now often passed its locked doors, perhaps forgetting the tragedy for the Oliphants too, in having to close down.

How the world had changed! It had happened quite suddenly. The oil wells simply dried up. No more wellingtons: it had been a terrible blow to the Major. Of course everything else had collapsed too. Machines of every kind were idle; silent; wrapped in sheets. Cars were a thing of the past, almost. The vicar had walked. It is what everyone did to get anywhere!

Meanwhile Audrey was caught up in the delights of organ music. She watched, fascinated, as the high street butcher wielded the hand pump which had stood idle for generations: there was no power for the organ. The music flowed and she imagined it as it would be heard in the street through the opened church doors, sliding down the nooks and narrow passages where there was no sun and into the surrounding gardens, into the growing things where light streamed through orange and red petals; and bright-eyed birds gorged themselves with insects which were multiplying over the face of the earth; into the washing which hung on the lines unable to dry; into the kitchens where people stood cooking the midday meal over wood fires, or methane gas stoves, if they were lucky; making puddings, thinking of a world without oil.

Audrey was suddenly brought back to reality by the sound of the vicar's voice. She felt nervous for him, because he kept on making comical mistakes in his sermons. She hoped he'd get through it well this Sunday.

~

The vicar had seemed fretful for some minutes before he was due to start his sermon. He clasped his hands on his stomach, speaking carefully.

'Friends,' he said, 'life goes on without the motor-car. We have discovered that! It goes on without fast food and television. Without the good things. For most of us, at least!' he added, taking care to look high up and straight over the Oliphants, whom he knew very well had recently swapped a pair of wellingtons for a case of pickles and two sides of bacon with a poor pensioner who preferred a near-empty larder to the abomination of wet feet.

It was a good beginning. But the congregation was waiting, the young and the old alike, for the first distressing signs of discomfiture and confusion. It was like a wave being held back; a wave of laughter, loosening, ready to break over him. It was never outright laughter. When he had preached a few Sundays ago, little Dolly Parkin had stood up and rushed to the aisle, making violent noises, and had apparently collapsed before being half-carried out by her mother. People stared hard up at the vicar, mouths open, eyebrows raised in delight.

'Now we see, don't we,' he said, 'we see that the things we grook for tanted ...'

He sweated. The held-in waves of laughter threatened to destroy him.

Desperately he tried to regain the order of the words. 'Thoing dimple sings. Doing ...' he said. 'Simple things, like walking.' He paused.

'Simple things ...' he repeated. He was talking freely now. There was that nasty little Pugh boy leering up at him in the fifth row, waiting for another slip. Still it was better for the boy that he was in church, better than frog-squashing. So many frogs these days. Frogs everywhere.

'We have ailed,' he said, coming to a violent stop. 'The fearth,' he muttered, 'We have failed ...' he said.

What did it mean, anyway? thought Audrey, making an effort to think seriously and so prevent a spasm of laughter. Trying to say we had not looked after the earth, the trees, the air. Too many aerosols, cars, all sorts of things. Everyone knew it.

'Refrigerators,' said the vicar, taking everyone by surprise. 'And we have filled the earth with kin tans, rubbish, haven't we?' he went on.

Then it was all over. His hands swept nervously over his neck. His eyebrows were soaked and his eyes stung.

'Depart in peace,' he said shortly afterwards, feeling decidedly weakened, more so than usual after a sermon.

~

As the congregation filed past they shook the vicar's hand. A few gathered outside in small groups in the hazy sunlight, swatting at the insects, and now laughing freely.

The vicar spoke to them all with ease. He enquired after people's health. Talking like this would be easy for days in a row, until the next sermon. He did not know why it was. In the street, anywhere, he was all right; having chats about growing carrots and onions; looking into prams.

He was wondering about all this as the Oliphants began to file past. Audrey came up to him. He watched her young face with pleasure; her golden hair drawn back so tight, it pulled the skin by her blue eyes. She smiled at him, trying not to look at his feet. The vicar had taken her hand and smiled too. Although as a rule he never had speech difficulties outside the pulpit, he now turned to a friend who was visiting him from another parish, saying, 'You must meet Audrey, and Mrs Oliphant ... and this is Major Ollington. He makes wellyphants, you know, or at least,' he muttered, miserably, realising his mistake, but trying to ignore it, 'he used to, of course!'

2

Bernie Breaks the Law

Audrey opened her bedroom windows wide, taking care to draw the netting again. One or two frogs were clearing their throats. Getting ready.

Earlier she had tried to reason: 'Dad, why don't you give them all away?— not just a pair to the vicar, I mean everyone who wants them. You said money was no longer important.'

'You don't understand, my dear .... It isn't,' he had replied, 'but in exchange for those wellingtons, we can have anything we want.'

Downstairs her parents would already be nodding off in the silence, as they tried to spirit away the night without television. 'And how do you know, both of you, what I want?' she sighed, 'In fact ... do I?'

She put her candle by the bed and returned to the window, parting the netting slightly. One of those sudden winds had sprung up. And for a while there was no sound save for its wild hiss. Then she knew what she wanted, suddenly, like the way the wind had risen: it was to get out, to travel! The netting billowed and the candle-light danced and flared.

From the bushes below, a voice was calling, 'Cherry!' followed by a low whistle and an exasperated: 'Drat that dog!'

Audrey leaned out. 'Uncle Bernie! Wait. I'm coming down!'

Mary, the Oliphants' domestic help, was in the kitchen, already taking Mr Weismann's coat and pulling a dreadful face.

'Where have you been this time?' Audrey protested, 'Look at it! You're in an awful mess: honestly, Uncle!'

He scowled fiercely which he often did as a matter of habit, as if to disguise his kind heart.

'It can't be avoided,' he said, his heavy eyebrows wobbling.

'Oh come on! And where's Cherry?' Audrey asked.

'She'll turn up.'

'If that dog of yours is in the same state ...' said Mary.

'You do smell!' Audrey said.

'It's not by choice. Look,' he muttered, fumbling down his chest, 'you would too, if you had what appears to be an old fish head down your shirt.'

'And your hair!' shrieked Audrey, lifting her candle. 'It's filthy.'

'You exaggerate, just like your mother. Now, seriously, do you think I like this? Do you think I do it for fun?'

'All right, then, what's it all about, Uncle? It's not the first time!'

'One day I'll tell you.'

'I only hope Mum doesn't come in. And if she did it

would serve you right. She's already been saying she's ashamed of the way you look most of the time. '

'And you, how about you? Are you ashamed?'

'Well, maybe I'm not. You know I'm not!' Audrey said quietly.

'Now, look, Mr Weismann,' Mary said, going to the clothes rack, 'take the Major's coat and gardening trousers; he never uses them. Go on, take these out with you, clean yourself at the pond, and leave your clothes there. I'll see to everything in the morning, and then I'll bring them over when they're washed and dried. Although,' she added, 'sometimes I don't know why I bother.'

After changing into the Major's gardening clothes, Bernie set out through the streets of the town, for home. It was on the outskirts, on the long straight road that ran to Ossington Cross, towards the old municipal rubbish tip.

~

Small cafés opened when they could; cooking at midday when the power was on, and serving the food cold at night, although perhaps they managed to heat up a bowl of soup on a wood stove if they had come across some fuel. Sometimes customers brought in an armful of their own wood. Places like McDonald's could not have carried on in this way.

Hot food was not always available and lacked variety, although at Bernie's favourite café, Fellini's, it was different. It had been one of the first to reopen, and they were never short of fuel. People came in off the streets and ate good wholesome things like pigs' trotters, mixed vegetable soup, fried eggs and bacon and various spaghetti dishes, made on the premises, and at any time of the day.

Fellini's had been the first to offer sock-drying facilities. In the kitchen, in front of the wood stoves, Mr Fellini had placed a screen made from some old chicken wire. They did not have Environmental Health Officers any more, besides which, the heat was too good to miss. For 20p you could take off your socks and have them dried on the wire, while you ate some delicious pork chops and Italian-style bread. It was partly because of this sock drying that Fellini's was so popular; which in turn meant that there was always enough fuel being brought in. People longed for companionship and found it in Fellini's.

~

As soon as Bernie arrived home, he soaped himself thoroughly and had a cold bath; and before dressing he grasped Cherry, who had returned in the meantime, and washed her as well. He tried to put the thought of a cup of tea, dry socks, perhaps a plate of eggs and ham, out of his head, but could not! So he went to Fellini's. He longed for dry socks. Also he wished for happiness. But dry feet was the condition he longed for most.

Major Oliphant had never said: 'Look here, Bernie, here's a pair of size 9's. Just right for you. Want them?' Or: 'No, no, no, I don't want anything for them. We're brothers-in-law, aren't we?' Nothing had ever been said.

In Fellini's, Bernie settled at a table with just one tallow candle on it. Although there were candles everywhere in the Oliphant home, they were still difficult enough to come by, owing to the great demand. Most towns and villages had their own tallow candle makers, who used the hard fat from beef and mutton.

Bernie looked around happily at the people in the café. There were those who cupped their faces in their hands, elbows on the table, their foreheads and noses tipped with light. Others were in the shadows, sitting bolt upright. Yet more were lying on the benches. Plenty of them seemed peaceful enough as they murmured and ate and waited. Most had their socks off.

As Bernie stretched his toes under the table, he reflected on his position. He had taken out his old Bentley when it had grown dark enough and given it a good run. But he had the strangest feeling that he had been watched all the time as he went about his experiments. It would have been more than anyone's life was worth, to have been seen driving around. If he was caught, think of the disgrace for the Oliphants! Not that many people knew he was related. He thought: if I told Mr Fellini that I was Oliphant's brother-in-law, he wouldn't believe it. 'What, you!' Mr Fellini would say, 'You, Bernie!'

Only government cars were seen on the road now. The North Sea gas they used had been liquefied and stored in cylinders, and government men alone could use the precious liquid. Fire engines, ambulances, and sometimes a police car, used methane gas, carried in huge inflatable bags on top of the vehicle. They could only travel short distances.

Farmers were lucky. Most farms used horses but the bigger farms with dairy herds were allowed one tractor, since they were the main producers of methane gas;

using the slurry from cows, sugar beet, some straw
perhaps, in the lidded steel containers: the digesters.

Sitting in Fellini's, thinking of the day's events made
Bernie sweat; but it was not the heat alone. It was the
fear of what might happen if he was caught. To use an
ordinary car on private business; to travel without a
permit, for fun, was against the law. To break it meant
prison.

3

Dreams of Far Away Places

Being a year older than Audrey, the Inkpin boy, as the Major was apt to call him, knew the inside of the wellington factory as well as Audrey, if not better; for his father, George Inkpin, had been the production manager. Oliver had often seen the huge machines pressing the flood of hot plastic into wellington boots.

Now they were silent, covered with sheets to protect them from a leaking roof. Abandoned everywhere on the factory floor, just as they had been left on the last day, were the trolleys on which the wellingtons were taken from the machines to the benches, where the straggly bits of still-warm plastic had been trimmed off the tops of the boots and from the heels. Now days, after school, Oliver sometimes climbed through a broken basement window.

Testing the colours of the dyes, making sure the heat was just right; in fact doing all the things expected of a production manager, had given his father a purpose. But now life for his parent, without welly-making, seemed to have little meaning. His lanky body tripped going up steps. He had pains in his neck; he wrapped towels round his head to blot out the sound of frogs at night. Not working with wellies any more, he was like a stone bouncing and spinning and breaking; falling out of sight.

'You'd think he'd find something else to interest him,' Oliver Inkpin said later to his friend, adding: 'I hope I don't get like that!'

'I'm sure you won't, Olly,' Audrey assured him. 'My father's just as bad. It's all he thinks about ... his wellies!'

They were walking on the straight road out of town, towards Bernie's. Already they were worn out, and now they sat under a hedge. Wild strawberries glittered bright red amongst the fallen twigs. Doves droned and flopped from tree to tree, as if they, too, felt the heat. Beyond the hedge, fat hens poked around in a field for fallen seed.

'The way your dad feels,' said Audrey, creeping further back into the shade, 'is the same with a lot of people. They can't take being without things: television, cars. And there's the lights with nothing happening when you switch on.'

'If only we could get out of here,' said Oliver. 'To really travel again: think of it!'

'Oh, don't!' sighed Audrey. 'Perhaps that's it, most of all: missing travelling. It's the thought of being stuck here.' Audrey hugged her knees. 'My parents haven't changed, you know. With all that's happened; all of us being in the same boat: they still think they're important and special, my dad, in particular.'

Oliver said nothing, his eyes looking browner than usual.

'At least I don't think I'm someone special,' she said.

He looked at her, then catching her glance, grinned, saying: 'Well, who says you are?'

Coming back into town, they felt the stares, the envy. 'Nice wellies,' someone muttered, adding: 'It's all right for some!'

'I shouldn't take any notice,' said Oliver, stumbling. He was becoming lanky, like his father.

'Oh sometimes I hate wellingtons! I mean, you can't blame them. Also the way my dad is swapping them ... People will exchange almost anything. It's almost robbery.'

'I wouldn't say that,' Oliver replied, rubbing his close-cut hair.

'And yet, d'you know that Bernie has no wellingtons? It's pretty awful, really. He's related for heaven's sake! And he's too proud to ask.'

'Families are like that.'

~

As they left, each for their own home, Mrs Oliphant, who was in town, having managed to escape from the Major for the afternoon, saw them. And there was Oliver swinging his arms about, and Audrey slouching a little, it seemed to her. It was something she had noticed lately, but which the Major had not. Not that Henry observed anything, she mused bitterly, unless it was to do with wellingtons!

~

Rather than stay in the house alone, the Major had made his way to the church, which he often did, to stand by Sir Edwin where he drummed his fingers on his ancestor's statue, in thought. The fact is he also wanted to be away from home and in the cool air of the church! How he longed for the cold air of winter; for crumpets and butter and strawberry jam by the fire; for a winter that was bitter cold! But the climate had changed. And people had changed! They simply gave up; look at George Inkpin!

As for the ex-workers, why, none of them gave him as much as a nod; as if it was his fault!

The welly-trimmer, Bessie Ottershaw, for example; she had taken to looking at him straight in the eye, when they passed in the street. Straight through with not a word. Afterwards it felt as if a plum stone was lodged in his head.

He paced up and down the aisle. Cool; very well, it was! But it made no difference to his thoughts, his worries, his little perplexities. He could not escape from anything. Also, people were not respectful, and that didn't help.

The Inkpins still treated him with respect: the boy, Oliver, and Mrs Inkpin and George Inkpin, of course. They could hardly do anything else. Only last week he'd given them Chinese ginger, maple syrup, a silver plated candlestick and some sugar tongs; being some of the things he had taken in exchange for a pair of wellingtons. It had obviously infuriated Audrey. Strange child. Difficult thing, growing up. Didn't see things properly.

The Major was delighted to look after the Inkpins like

this; for George had known how to mix colours; how to manage it all, whereas he, the Major, knew nothing about that side of it, except how to nod at people in the factory.

Without George, the Major would have got the colours wrong. Pig farmers would have worn pink wellies. Solicitors out for a stroll by the river on a Sunday would have had to make do with mottled-looking boots the colour of old bananas.

Oh yes, when there was power again, he would need George Inkpin. He had no doubt about that, if by then, of course, there was enough rubber to go round. There still would not be any plastic.

The Major stood by Sir Thomas in the silent church, his hand resting upon the knight's cold marble chest.

Oliphants! thought Major Oliphant with pride. What strength it gave one to be an Oliphant! How weak Inkpin was to give in to despair; yet so many did! How foolish the vicar with his 'wellyphants', although it had given him an idea. Even if there was no plastic, one day things would pick up a little. And, thought the Major, what about then using 'Wellyphants' as a trade name? Pairs of wellyphants! Wellyphants for your little boy, madam? A pair of size 2; hurry it along! Wellyphants for the lady.

He patted Sir Thomas affectionately, and nodded at Lady Judith. 'A splendid idea!' he muttered.

~

That evening, Mary had made her final retreat to the kitchen after coming in three times and saying: 'Will that be all, then?'

'I'm sure she does it to annoy,' said Mrs Oliphant. 'Henry, when are you going to have words with her?'

'She's trying to look after us,' Audrey said.

'She doesn't mean it. Disrespectful,' the Major grumbled.

'I think she means it,' said Audrey.

'Ever since you had to attend the town school your attitude has changed,' her mother said. 'Frankly the sooner we can use the car to get you back to boarding school, the better it will be.'

'I can't think of anything more horrid than going back to St Cuthbert's,' said Audrey. 'And you won't take me in our car, Mum: we'll never use it again. When there's power from fusion, we'll all have electric cars and we'll just plug in at garages to recharge the batteries.'

'So they say,' said Mrs Oliphant, 'But I'm talking about your behaviour.'

'Quite right!' said the Major. 'And there's another thing, Audrey, we don't want you seeing so much of your uncle.'

'Why ever not, Dad?' Audrey asked incredulously.

'Little incidents. Too many of them. Earlier on today I saw him going in the back way with a bundle of clothes. Mary was taking them off the kitchen table and hanging them up behind the door. They were my gardening coat and trousers.'

'He's been wearing your trousers? How disgusting!' said Mrs Oliphant.

'Oh, I don't know,' said the Major.

'For you, dear.'

'D'you both mean I shouldn't see Uncle Bernie?'

'There'll be family occasions, I'm sure,' said the

Major.'I just don't want you spending too much time over there. Your Uncle doesn't behave like one of us. Doesn't even look like one of us ... decidedly mucky.'

'He can't help it,' said Audrey.

'Of course he can; I've never heard such nonsense!' said Mrs Oliphant.

'And there's Oliver. Surely you could pick more suitable friends? You are an Oliphant, you know.'

'And don't forget it, my dear,' said the Major.

'You can't mean it, Dad!'

'Of course you're an Oliphant,' he insisted.

'Oh, I know I am,' said Audrey.

'Oliver's father, splendid fellow. If it all starts up again, dread to think what I'd do without him,' he said, after a pause.

'Yes, but we're talking about Oliver, Henry,' said Mrs Oliphant firmly. 'Slouching about in town.'

'We'd been to Uncle Bernie's, but he wasn't in. We were tired, that's all.'

~

Lying on her bed, hands clenching, Audrey thought: If only I could get away for a while! But where to?

She remembered those few years ago, when travel had been possible. When it was not yet a crime. What would it be like now? With the earth as it was? Now, tonight? With no lights anywhere; past the fields, white with mist; past the rooks settled in the dark trees for sleep.

4

A Brilliant Idea

One or two people had mentioned to the Major that it was too hot for wellingtons anyway; too hot and sweaty. He wondered: were they just trying to hide their envy; pretending they did not care? The trick was to have a pair which were not too tight; then the foot glided in. Of course that was it; not at all sweaty! And had not the insides of all his wellingtons been coated with his very own Sweat Linings and Absorbers (Patented), known as S.L.A.P.s in the trade?

But what, if for all that, when the revival came with the new-age power, people had got out of the habit? What if people had gone off them? What if pig farmers, for instance, simply washed their feet before sitting down to breakfast?

Yet there would always be winter, he assured himself; not the same as it used to be, but cooler, none the less. Wind in the trees and chimney pots; rain yelping down drains. Cool, and wet, and ideal for wellies!

Bessie Ottershaw, shivering, her heart laden with

hatred for the Major; yes he could see it, he could feel it; even she longed for wellies! The bowl in which she ignorantly grew that geranium was worth a fortune. But she was not to know it, and if he bided his time, he would be able to have it for just one pair; such was her desire, and it was a common desire ... for wellingtons.

~

The Major went from room to room, looking for Priscilla. Finding her, he said, 'Ah, my dear.'

'Henry?'

'There will be a revival of power, dear. You may be certain of that.'

'I know you believe that, and I respect your opinion,' she said uncertainly.

'But I doubt if there will be enough rubber for everything; not in my lifetime anyway. Now,' he said, settling down, 'people have wellyphants in sheds. I'm thinking about plastic wellyphants, you understand. Take Bessie Ottershaw.'

'Please, Henry!'

'I've seen it. I had to go over there a few weeks ago. She grows geraniums, you know. In her shed; guess what I saw? Apart from a welly trimming knife which she had no doubt stolen ...'

'If we're going to talk about footwear, dear, d'you think for my sake, as an act of consideration,' she said, her voice rising dangerously, 'we could refer to the articles as "wellingtons"?'

'Oh very well. Yes, very well.' She was coming out in a rash, and he was now watching it rudely. 'You are not troubled, dear?' he asked.

'Not at all. You were saying?'

'Yes, wellingtons, then. Guess what? Bessie has got not just one pair of old wellies in her shed. She's got four pairs! All of them no good. They're absolutely full of cracks and holes and in one of them I noticed an old blackbird's nest. Whole place stank of onions hanging up, balls of string; that sort of thing. People keep things in sheds. And what is more,' he said, getting up and pacing in front of her, 'there are some things people don't look at twice, not in a certain way that is, before throwing them away. Bottles for example.'

'I always used to put them in the bottle bank, when they were collecting,' she said weakly.

'It's got nothing to do with bottle banks. What I'm saying is that people get rid of some things and keep others. Don't you understand?'

'I think so,' she replied, beginning to scratch.

'Now, wellingtons,' he said, in consideration for her, 'people having worn them; having put them on, and then taken them off all that number of times, become fond of them. It's human nature. Like old sweaters and things; they do not want to throw them away.'

'Besides which,' she suggested, 'they would have been difficult to put in a rubbish bag, as they would keep springing up, making it difficult to close the top.'

'Yes, a useful point,' said the Major. 'My dear,' he continued, 'there must be hundreds, no, thousands of wellyphants within easy reach of us.'

'You said ...' She started to scratch again.

'Yes, they're wellyphants. Sorry, but they are. It's a splendid tradename and I intend to register it.'

She continued to look uncertain, even drab, in one of

her strange miseries.

'I must use the name and believe in it,' he insisted. 'Ever seen those poor fellows selling brushes at the door? Eyes drooping. Tips of noses red in the summer and blue in the winter. At the mercy of the weather. They believe in their brushes. Cleaning nasty nooks. Lots of people can't resist the talk, simply because these fellows believe in their product. It's simple, really.'

'I suppose so,' she said with resignation.

She had not even waited to hear what he intended; simply moved off, without a word!

Still, lots of people were feeling irritable and had minor ailments. Poor Priscilla, he thought. The vicar was a further example; his sermons were a disgrace! Only a few days ago the major had felt obliged to speak to him.

'Not faith, is it, vicar?' he had asked. 'No problems with it, I mean; there aren't any little passages in the Bible you don't believe in? I knew a subaltern, found he didn't believe in killing any more. Tried to say "fire!", but couldn't. Entire battery wiped out.'

'Nothing like that,' the vicar had answered.

~

At any rate, there were little passages in the Bible which the Major believed in more passionately than others. Take Genesis. About the fishes and the fowls being man's to do with what he liked. And why not the minerals, he thought; the timber, the rivers, the blessed lot? Find, mine, pump, heat, mould, and trim it!

Indeed: find it! Now it made better sense than ever before!

If he waited for the rubber from the new plantations which were no doubt being planted, why, he'd be an old man! Priscilla would have lost all her own teeth.

Other manufacturers had had the same idea, quite some time before the Collapse. Dunlop Footwear, in Liverpool; he had gone there to have a look. But no one had really done much about it.

He would collect up all the plastic wellies, in the town and round about, as far as he could. Wretched business it would be, with horse and cart; get someone else to do it! Rewards here and there. He would make Inkpin chief collector. And he would go to the heart of the enemy; Corporal Ottershaw, that sort of thing. Create agitation, promotion, stress. All of that.

He would build piles of wellingtons, of wellyphants! He would recycle them!

He wanted to find Priscilla again; to tell her; but then thought: too much for the old girl; all at once.

~

As for Priscilla, she had gone into town with Audrey, where they had seen Bernie in the High Street. 'What do you mean by taking his trousers?' she demanded, in the full hearing of those on the pavement. 'Why do you do these things, Bernie?'

'Mum, please!' Audrey had whispered fiercely.

But ignoring her, Mrs Oliphant continued, 'If it wasn't for Henry, where would you be? Who lent you the money for your house?'

Bernie did not answer. He seemed for an instant unable to do so. His eyebrows shook. His mouth was set and he stared with fatigue.

5

Bernie's Secret

As soon as Audrey could, she went to see Bernie; frequently stopping on the way out of town and resting in the shade of the hedges. She was angered at her parents' treatment of him. She was troubled about his appearance.

A horse and cart lumbered out of the mist into the sun; the driver spread across the wooden seat, asleep. She climbed up the moist bank from the roadside into the woods, taking the short cut.

'Uncle!' she called, opening the back door; and then a moment later: 'You look so tired. That was an awful thing to say!'

'About the house? But it's true of course. Without your father's help, where would I be?'

'In a room somewhere. I don't know.'

'Look,' he said, tapping his chest, 'I've got self respect. I'm an inventor! I have a house, a laboratory. And I thank your father for this. Where would I be? your mother asks. I tell you, in a poky little room, like you said, not looking after myself, miles away from you, Angel, and everybody. No Mary to iron my shirts. And if I didn't have my inventions, I'd go crazy, and also I owe that to your father! In other words,' he smiled, 'it's not so bad; I can put up with a little criticism.'

'All right, but he hasn't even given you a new pair of wellingtons.'

'So: and if he hasn't? But I still don't like to hear you talk like that about him.'

'I just wish he'd give them away. I've lost all my friends except Oliver ... they're envious.'

'Besides, I don't need wellies. There's Fellini's.'

'What's at Fellini's?'

'They dry my socks.'

'That doesn't sound very satisfactory, although I agree wellies aren't everything.'

'Look,' said Bernie gently, 'because of what I'm doing, my inventions, things will look up for me.'

'I'm sure they will,' she said lightly.

'I can't tell you, yet.'

'I don't mind,' said Audrey.

'About my inventions.'

'Yes, of course. I'm not all that curious,' she said, trying to sound bored.

'You must make allowances for your parents.'

'I know that.'

'I would tell you more about it, but not yet.'

'Don't worry, Uncle,' Audrey said.

House plants trailed in every direction, from ledges and shelves, over chests of drawers and bookcases. Audrey noticed that the cups and dishes were washed and stacked on the draining board.

Glancing at the heavily padlocked laboratory door next to the kitchen, Audrey said, 'Perhaps it would help if you didn't look as you do sometimes; with Mum and Dad I mean. I know it's not important, but they can't help themselves.'

'I am near the end of it,' he said quite unexpectedly.

'What are you at the end of?'

'It has been a particularly trying time, getting it right. And the conditions: those rubbish tips!'

'Mary knows what you're up to, doesn't she? She won't say anything, either.'

'If you don't know, then you're not involved; perhaps it's better that way. '

'She's been here, hasn't she? I'm glad Mary helps. She said you were a brave man.'

'I... a brave man? I think some of us have duties thrust upon us. There is no choice for me. Not with the world as it is.'

She thought: he will tell me, soon enough, for he is tired. He has had enough!

'I know you're inventing something important,' she said carelessly, 'but then you always were.'

On the table was a neat pile of shirts and underwear.

'She's even done the clothes,' he said. 'It was, of course, unusual for me to call at your house in that disgusting state. I can usually change here. It just happened that then I could not. No, normally she comes here to help with the washing; a little housework; and without her support ...'

'Tell me, Uncle!'

He took her hand. His own hand was barely larger than hers. His grey eyes were unsmiling. 'One day, soon perhaps, I will let you into my secret.'

'May I bring Oliver with me next time?'

'Of course. That's the Inkpin boy? Come to tea; let me see, next Saturday? It will have to be nettle tea. With lots of milk it's hard to tell the difference. And I'll have a sponge cake, plenty of new-laid eggs, too, and fresh bread.'

~

But the house had been empty on Saturday.

'We could wait,' suggested Oliver.

'I'm sure he's forgotten. He often does; with all sorts of things.'

'Is that where he experiments?' Oliver asked, pointing.

'He's even forgotten to lock the laboratory,' she replied. 'He must have a lot on his mind. Come on: let's go in!'

Looking at the cluttered benches, Oliver finally said: 'What a mess; what a ghastly mess!'

'In that respect Bernie's got problems,' Audrey sighed.

She gave the dog a piece of pork crackling from one of the dirty plates stacked in the kitchen and shook her head saying: 'Look at it. Just look. Mary has not been, obviously.'

They washed up and left.

On the way back they saw a government car pulled in off the road, into the shade. Instinctively they stepped back under the trees, walking silently on the moss, unseen.

The official government flag fluttered in the breeze.

Two overweight men dressed in suits with ties and white shirts, and with pasty-looking faces to match, had got out and were walking slowly up and down, trying to escape the heat.

After they had re-entered the car the uniformed driver checked the heavy wire grills over the side and rear windows. The front windscreen was also heavily protected.

As they drove off at speed, a horse and cart with a load of refuse travelling in the direction of the rubbish tip, shied in fright.

Audrey shivered. 'It's as if they come from another world,' she said.

~

The men who unloaded the carts hardly glanced at Bernie's lonely figure. Lately he had been a common enough sight at the tip, and passed for one of the gypsies who scavenged there, so dirty did he look.

He carried a long steel rod connected by wires to an instrument panel which was strapped over his shoulder. He slithered lightly over the grass-covered mounds of old rubbish, and across ditches full of frogs.

Once the ground seemed to swallow him up to his waist. Moving to a safe patch he carefully laid the rod by his side and picked the same sort of remnants from his body and hair that had so shocked Audrey.

Now and then he pushed the rod into the ground. When a green light glowed on the instrument panel, he marked the details in a notebook, together with a reading from the instruments.

He pushed the rod into the last hole, where he had

fallen, and sat down, smiling happily as the light glowed and the indicator reached maximum.

Then he carefully closed up the rod like he would a telescope and made his way out of the tip. A cloud of flies followed him.

'I have done it!' he gasped aloud. 'I have managed it! The experiments are over!'

Arriving home, Bernie noticed that the door to his laboratory was open. He closed and locked it, pausing for a moment. He suddenly had an uneasy feeling. But he shrugged this off and went for a cold bath. Afterwards he rinsed out the worst of the filth from his clothes, leaving the rest for Mary who was due the following day. In the kitchen he muttered: 'I could have sworn I didn't wash up ... but then I must have done. I have too much on my mind.'

He lay on his bed in the pale afternoon light, half-listening to the bees through his open window. Geraniums filled the window sill. Leaves which had dried and withered were strewn by the pots where they had fallen. Across the room, on a rope, hung shirts and underwear.

As he slept, his huge eyebrows twitched. When he turned over the twitching would cease for a while; but only to start again as did Cherry's leg when she sat down in a certain way.

~

Candles glowed from the windows of the terraces, and doors opened here and there as people started to gather on the streets. A government car had smashed its way through several tables which had been placed on the roadway outside cafés for street parties. Broken cups and bottles lay everywhere.

Workers had come in from the beet fields, from the hoeing, the stooping and cutting. The single evening bells from the churches had rung out. And then they too were silent.

Across the town from which had once risen the endless sound of traffic there could now be heard the ungovernable lowing of distant cattle. Occasionally the noise of laughter, of shouting, erupted from different parts of the town.

Fellini's was full as usual. For Bernie, as for many others, this was a marvellous gathering place. He had woken up refreshed and now sat at one of the tables.

The fact that most people were taking advantage of Mr Fellini's offer to dry socks and were sitting there with bare feet seemed to kindle the spirit of friendship between them.

Bernie had also taken a pair of socks off the line in his bedroom, and now handed both pairs to the waiter.

The soup tasted delicious: the crusty bread even better. Bernie thought of the forces against him: the government men; warnings about road travel; the threat of prison; the local people who watched him, ready for the slightest slip.

He imagined himself spinning down the desolate road beyond Ossington Cross in his old Bentley, lights off; guided by a powdering of light from the night sky.

And now at last he could say the experiment was over. The municipal tip was mapped; its volume of gas was known. His invention worked. He felt light-limbed with relief!

Now he needed some help. He could not manage it

alone any more; he knew that. There was some scuffling at an adjoining table; someone complaining that his socks had been scorched. Bernie took no notice.

His earlier doubts about allowing Audrey to become involved had vanished. Perhaps Oliver, too?

Next morning, unaware that he had already forgotten about the Saturday invitation, he sent a message inviting them to tea. He delivered it to the school rather than to Audrey's home, knowing something of the Oliphants' feelings, although not realising just how bad things now were between them.

6

S.N.I.F.F. and S.M.E.L.L.

'With my inventions ... using methane, I could travel; just think of it,' said Bernie, pouring himself a cup of nettle tea. 'More for you, Audrey? Oliver? It's a matter of taste: you like it or you don't.'

'Apart from the fact that you wouldn't be allowed to travel, why go to the trouble, Bernie?' Oliver asked. 'Everyone knows about methane.'

'Sure, it's easy enough to make the gas. No doubt you've seen the digesters outside the fire station ... you know; the containers into which the beet and artichokes and everything else is put, so that it rots down nicely and then gives off the gas?'

'So, if you can make methane some other way, perhaps; we already know it can be used ... What's so special in that?' asked Oliver.

'More cake?' replied Bernie. Cherry, lying on the carpet, swivelled her eyes to look at him and sighed, head in paws.

'I want to travel; to go over the face of the earth,'

Bernie said simply.

'But you wouldn't be allowed to,' insisted Audrey.

'Not just down the road, a bit. For miles and miles; don't you remember the feeling?' he said, ignoring her objection.

'Oh, yes!' she replied dreamily, 'but that's not the point.'

'Ambulances and fire engines use methane. They carry it in those gas-bags, don't they?' said Oliver,' and I've seen tractors on some of the farms.'

'It's the big farmers who keep the digesters full, so yes, of course for them it's legal, too,' Bernie said. 'For anyone else it's not legal to travel. For me it's not legal; already people are watching me. But I tell you something else; they can't go far, these fire engines and so on; just here around Newtown, and to Ossington, maybe. Then to make another journey they have to refill those huge bags they carry on top, with more gas.

'And one digester isn't enough. You need lots: fire stations have two or three dozen, all being filled up from the farms. Every time there's a fire they have to fill up the digester they took the gas from. Now, if I, for example, build myself a digester and fill it, I have to wait three weeks for the microbes to work and then there's only enough methane for a trip to somewhere like Ossington.'

'You've made your point, Bernie; so what's the invention for?' asked Oliver.

'In a moment, I tell you,' said Bernie, 'don't rush me.'

'But however you do it, you're not allowed to!' said Audrey with increasing impatience.

'Look,' said Bernie, 'the government cars don't use

methane gas in its natural form, like the ambulances do; they carry cylinders of liquefied gas. On one cylinder they can go a hundred miles or more.'

'Yes, and you're not a government car,' persisted Audrey.

'I know I'm not,' said Bernie, 'and furthermore, you'll ask: why don't the ambulances use it then?'

'I was going to,' admitted Oliver.

'There's simply not enough of it,' said Bernie. 'For a start you need huge quantities of gas in order to make liquefying worth while; I mean like what remains of the North Sea gas. That's where the liquefying is done: where the gas comes in from the North Sea. And it's got to be liquefied to be transported. Most of it goes to the power stations. What they can spare is put into cylinders for government transport.'

'And your inventions, Uncle Bernie?'

'What I've invented is a number of things, all to do with the liquefying of gas, but on a small scale.'

'So, where do you get the gas from?' she asked.

'Not from using digesters! There wouldn't be enough of it.' Bernie smiled. 'I get it from rubbish tips.'

'I begin to see,' said Audrey.

'Mind you it's not ready to use like the digester gas; it has to be cleaned.'

'All right, Uncle. So you've liquefied it and you can go long distances. What happens if you meet a government car? What about the police?'

'Once I've made several journeys and proved it all works, I will go to the government officials, and I do a deal so it's legal for me.'

'I'm not so sure about that,' said Audrey.

'Well, I am,' said Bernie. 'After all, my inventions would be a great help to the authorities. Liquefying gas for the fire engines, think of it!'

'You might become famous,' said Oliver.

'Who cares about fame? I don't! Now ... my problem has been to find a way to discover this gas on the tips and then to extract and liquefy it for use in the car. Luckily I was able to get all the engineering work done before the Collapse. This device,' he continued, wiping his hands carefully on the table cloth, and then holding up the instrument he had earlier used on the tip, 'is for finding where the gas is. A lot of adjustments had to be made. I couldn't get it right at the beginning. Then, yesterday, it all seemed to come together. It is a beautiful-looking thing, is it not?'

'Yes, but what is it?' asked Oliver.

'He's coming round to it,' said Audrey.

'What it does,' said Bernie, 'is to show the presence of methane gas, by means of these battery-powered dials. It is an extremely delicate sensor, which has taken me years to perfect, all of which is encased in this steel-tipped spear. To answer your question, I find it more agreeable to give it a name and then if people like you ask me what it is, I can say, "I will tell you with pleasure. It is a S.N.I.F.F." '

'You've certainly put a lot of work into it,' said Audrey.

'What do you think I've been doing these last few months? I know our town rubbish tip better than anyone. I know where all the choice bits are. The really smelly places.'

'And that accounts for your appearance!'

Flecks of sunlight filtered in past the window plants. Bernie's eyebrows danced. 'And S.N.I.F.F.s will catch on. Once the law says it's all right. Once these government people see sense, S.N.I.F.F.s would be in great demand.'

'But how would you make more of them? There's no power,' said Audrey.

'I mean when we get the new energy,' Bernie replied.

'Then we won't need methane,' pointed out Oliver. 'Not with fusion power and electric cars.'

'My dear friend,' said Bernie, 'That's my small contribution to the Earth. When the new age power is here, we will need to use up as much methane from our rubbish tips as we can. Using it for fuel causes less harm to the atmosphere than just letting the gas leak out, which is what it does, over the years. Using methane will be like scavenging; like picking up bits of paper; keeping the earth OK. And in the meantime, as the inventor, I will be able to go anywhere!'

'That would be wonderful,' Audrey said, trying to keep calm.

'We need proof,' said Bernie.

~

'So, what does S.N.I.F.F. stand for?' asked Oliver.

'It is,' said Bernie, 'my Secret and Neat Invention for Finding Foulness.'

'That doesn't sound very scientific,' said Audrey.

'That part of it isn't,' admitted Bernie. 'I like Sniff as a word, and it seemed to be the right one in this case.'

'And why are you telling the two of us, Uncle?'

'Because I need help ... someone I can trust. There's

Mary. But if she were caught she would be imprisoned. Heavens knows what!'

'Yes, but what about me and Oliver?'

'You can run faster than Mary, and besides they would let you off. You're too young to spend the night in a police cell.'

'Don't you know the terrible trouble I'd be in at home?' asked Audrey. 'And what about Oliver?'

'I shouldn't have asked it.'

There was a long silence.

'I got carried away,' said Bernie. 'I needed someone to read the S.N.I.F.F. instruments while I unwind the nozzle from the car.'

'What nozzle?'

'It doesn't matter,' said Bernie. He tipped the remains of his cake on the carpet. Cherry ate it and kept on licking the carpet afterwards, getting some of the worn bits in her mouth.

'Do you think she likes it?' asked Oliver.

'I suppose so,' said Bernie, then: 'The nozzle on the end of a long pipe ... I put the nozzle into S.N.I.F.F. and rush back to the car and switch on.'

'A shortage of hands,' said Audrey. 'You really do need some help, don't you?'

'What do you call the thing in the car?' asked Oliver.

'What do you call, what do you call!' said Bernie, shaking his head. 'I tell you what it does. It liquefies the gas. The engine runs on this liquefied gas.'

'Is that all?' said Oliver.

'It's enough,' said Bernie. 'And I call it S.M.E.L.L. What d'you think of that?

'You choose some odd names, Uncle.'

'This is a serious business, what I am doing. Why not a little fun with it? Anyway, it's logical. It's a Stinking Methane Extractor Liquefier and Lozenger. I know that pure methane has no smell, but there are other gases mixed in with it. It varies.'

'And it makes methane lozenges as well? That's fantastic,' said Oliver.

'Not yet, and not exactly,' said Bernie. 'I haven't time to mess around with lozenges. Time is not on our side.'

'Then why do you say it does it, if it doesn't?' asked Audrey.

'I suppose, if you twist my arm, I have to admit, because it spells better; that's all. Forget this lozenging and come into the garage and have a look under the lid of my old Bentley. Tomorrow we'll go to the tip; you'd like that?'

'Rather!' said Oliver uncertainly, glancing at Audrey.

7

And Not to Mention W.H.I.F.F.!

The following day it rained. When it stopped, the town gardens and surrounding fields were filled with birdsong, shrilling above the sound of water which moved in the drains and ditches. Within minutes the steam had started to rise from the buildings and fields.

'I thought maybe you weren't going to manage it,' said Bernie. 'What are those sandwiches?'

'Pork and pickle. Mary made them for us.' Audrey replied.

'Good. And I see you're not wearing your best clothes.'

'Mary said I was to wash and change in the kitchen, and leave the dirty clothes outside. She said she'd see to it.'

'Without Mary ...' he began.

'And,' continued Audrey, 'she said she hoped I knew what I was doing!'

'Well, do you? And you, Oliver?'

'Even if my parents knew, they wouldn't mind,' he said, 'but I can see it's better they don't know. Not yet, at any rate.'

'When my trial runs are completed, everything will be above board, like it should be,' Bernie assured them.

'We both know what we're doing,' Audrey said. 'And your work is very important; anyone can see that.'

'Good,' said Bernie. 'And I must say, I'm glad your mother let you come here for tea and supper. Next time I see her I'll thank her.'

'I shouldn't mention it,' Audrey said. 'Please don't.'

'Why not?'

'Oh, I don't know. Just a feeling I've got,' she said awkwardly, remembering what her father had said to her about contact with Uncle Bernie.

'The only problem is the ground on the tip will be in such a mess after all that rain,' Bernie said, looking out the window. 'Look, I don't want to disappoint you, but the demonstrations with S.N.I.F.F. could be given another day. How about tomorrow, if it dries up a bit?'

'Oh dear,' said Audrey.

'Today, I could explain the dials again. All right, maybe we've done enough of that,' he said as he watched their faces. 'But I tell you what, when it gets dark we could go for a drive. Your parents know where you are. The sky is clear, and the mist is thin enough,' he said, looking through a gap in the geranium-filled window, where the condensation was streaming off the glass on to the sill. He added: 'And what's more, there's enough fuel.'

'Won't we be seen?' asked Audrey.

'Not the way I do it,' said Bernie. 'A short cut out of here, away from the town, through the woods and out on to the road to Ossington Cross.'

'That'll be fine, as far as we're concerned,' said

Audrey. 'The very thought of travel; even if it's just down the road ...!'

~

Before they reached the road, Bernie switched off the lights. In the distance, they could see the black shapes of the town buildings, and ahead of them, the fields and hedges, and the long straight road to Ossington, glimmering in the moonlight.

'It's magnificent! What a night!' said Bernie.

'What do you want us to do?' asked Audrey.

'Nothing. Just sit tight.'

'Won't we be seen?' queried Oliver.

'On that road there's only Jim Hood, an old pig farmer, and his wife, Mabel. And we'll keep our lights off, anyway.'

'No lights, Uncle: you can't mean it!' Audrey cried.

'Oh yes, I do. How else d'you think I've been conducting experiments without being found out?'

Mary's warning 'I hope you know what you're doing!' tumbled through her head.

'But Uncle!'

To their left a chorus of frogs broke the silence. Bernie smiled gently at them as they leaned forward from the back seat. 'Now I will show you a little invention of mine. And another time, maybe you trust me. It's powered by my super-batteries ... and with a little help from the generator.'

'What generator?' asked Oliver.

'It doesn't matter what generator. But look, I tell you what it does.'

'What do you call it?' asked Oliver.

'First of all,' said Bernie, firmly, 'I will tell you what it does. That screen in front of you here near the left-hand door is a heat imager. In other words, if I turn on this switch, it shows the presence of people, voles, jack-daws, horses, anything which is warm and alive and ahead of us on the road.'

'I know,' said Oliver. 'Police used to use them in their helicopters to find criminals.'

'That's right,' said Bernie. 'I borrowed the idea and developed it a little.'

'Why not!' agreed Audrey.

'So, what do you call it then?' asked Oliver.

'But Uncle, what about the frogs? They're cold-blooded and won't show up,' interrupted Audrey. 'There must be hundreds on the road. Are you just going to run over them?'

'Look,' he said in hurt tones, 'can you imagine me, Bernie Weismann, allowing such a thing to happen?'

'I'm sorry, Uncle.'

'So, how do you get over it?' asked Oliver.

'I will tell you what I call it.'

'I dread to think,' said Audrey.

'A ... W.H.I.F.F.'

'So, all right,' said Oliver, 'what does it stand for?

'Good,' said Bernie, smiling, 'it's Weismann's Heat Imager Fitted with Frog-Scoopers.

He pulled a lever. 'Let's have a look,' he said and the three of them got out and went to the front of the car.

'It shoots them back into the side of the road,' he said simply, 'with the aid of rotating brushes.'

Audrey took his hand.

'It is marvellous,' she said gently. 'I should have

known better.'

'The wire screen is in case we hit something else on the road, like a table, which, not being warm, wouldn't show on the screen. The government cars have screens too, because of the habit people have these days of sitting out in the streets.'

'Why d'you think they do that?' Audrey asked.

'People like having street parties; also it's because of the government cars. People can show their defiance; they do it to annoy. You'll find they're usually old tables anyway.'

'And who wants to sit in a gloomy old room, in the candle-light?' said Oliver.

'That's right,' replied Bernie. 'But there's nothing like that on the road to Ossington Cross.'

~

Jim Hood and his wife, Mabel, were in the kitchen.

'You tek your wellies off afore you sit at this table, for supper, Jim Hood,' she said.

'They've cracks in 'em. They're split. Pulling 'em off all the time will only make 'em worse!'

'I won't have the farm in my kitchen,' said Mabel, turning over some fine-looking sausages in a pan on a glowing wood-burning stove.

'I'm keepin' 'em on,' he said.

'Then you'll have yours outside. Outside on the road for all I care, just like the fancy people do in the town; you'll see if you don't!'

'So I will!' he said, in a temper, taking the table with him. 'I'll be back for me sausages.'

Disgusted, she emptied the entire pan-full on his

plate. 'There!' she shouted. 'Take your dinner with you!'

Jim put the table on the road and walked back into the house, grumbling. He returned a moment later with the sausages, a hunk of bread, and a chair.

'Now,' he muttered to himself, getting to his feet once again. 'Darn it, blessed if I ain't forgot the blumin' mustard!'

In the meantime, Bernie, Audrey and Oliver sped down the road. Looking at the heat-imager, Oliver said: 'What's that on the W.H.I.F.F.?'

'Mice, probably,' said Bernie. 'They'll get out of the way.'

A moment later there was a splintering crash. They had crashed into Jim's table and his plate of sausages, though they didn't know it.

The car stopped fifty metres on, and a white-faced Bernie walked to the front.

Audrey had covered her face with both hands.

'Oh no, no!' Oliver was saying.

Bernie came back tossing some bits of hot sausage from hand to hand.

'Take them,' he said, licking his fingers.

Further down the road they stopped, turned round and waited.

'Give it some time,' said Bernie. 'He'll have gone indoors and we can get back unseen. One day I'll call in and explain.'

'The sausages are delicious,' said Audrey.

'Gosh, yes,' Oliver agreed.

'Just the right amount of seasoning,' said Bernie.

'And W.H.I.F.F. works beautifully,' Audrey added with a smile.

8

Danger at the Tip

'It looks like a grocery shop, dear,' said Mrs Oliphant, viewing the spare bedroom which was stacked with an overflow of goods the Major had taken in from the town and surrounding countryside in exchange for wellies.

'We have too many things, too many groceries; can't you see? When is this going to stop?'

'It has stopped, Priscilla.'

'I'm glad! Of course we've done very well out of it. I only hope people don't think they've paid too high a price. At times, I must say, I do wonder.'

'They've got wellies in return and the peace of mind that comes with dry feet, and that's beyond price. You can't put a figure to it like you can with a pound of peas or a pig's trotter.'

'And this,' she waved at the filled room, 'it has stopped, you say?'

'Enough is enough,' said the Major.

'You don't know how glad I am. There have been moments when I have felt that wellies and what you can swap them for have preyed on your mind.'

'At times, my dear, you do talk the most awful non-sense. I am an Oliphant. We make, or rather we made and one day we shall start making again, our quite wonderful wellyphants. *Olifans vincit omnia*' he said, quoting the family motto. 'Does that mean anything to you?'

'Not a lot.'

' "The Oliphants conquer all",' he said in an aston-ished voice. 'Surely you know that!'

'Of course I know it. I mean as far as I am personally concerned it cannot mean quite so much. I have taken your name. I was a Weismann.'

'My dear, surely you now consider yourself an Oliphant? And wellyphants are my life! The source of all our comfort. How can such things prey on me, as you say?'

'I should not have said it ...'

'And good old George Inkpin, he's been drawing plans for a welly chopper. In consideration for your feelings I will not call them wellyphants. It's a simple thing. Blades on it. Goes round and round. They had them in Liverpool, before the Collapse. Ear-splitting noise. And he's also doing drawings of a shaker. So you wouldn't say it's preying on his mind, would you? All the bits of wellies, about the thickness of marmalade peel.'

'Why, Henry?' said Mrs Oliphant.

'Why what? Marmalade? To give you an idea of course. It's better than going around talking about milli-metres. Surely I told you I intend to recycle them? When the new-age power, the fusion power is here, of course.

We'll shake the bits. Straightforward, isn't it? Chop up the old wellies. Make new wellies. First of all shake out the linings from the chopped bits of the old wellies. Bits of sock and chicken manure ...'

'You make it sound so; I don't know,' she said, scratching.

'I've started with Inkpin. Going around looking in sheds for old wellies. Doing a survey. "Excuse me, madam, I'm Oliphant. This is Inkpin. Any wellies under your stairs? In your dear little garden shed? I see you have a pair by the rubbish bin. Can't get 'em in the sacks; tops keep popping up? That's just what my wife said".' After a pause he added, 'It puts them at their ease.'

'I'm glad there are some people upon whom you have that effect,' said Mrs Oliphant.

'And George is good at it, too. Mind you, we're only getting information, then we'll make a plan for collecting them into small dumps and horse and cart them on to the Oliphant Footwear car park. There's a fortune waiting for me, in people's unwanted wellies.

'But if only we could get out beyond Ossington, into all the towns and cities, collecting up old wellies ... now, before anyone else does it! If only there was some way we could legally use our lorries! But I suppose it's better than nothing; what we're doing, George and I.'

'I do wish Audrey wasn't seeing so much of their boy. Last night she stayed at the Inkpins' for supper. I worry because of the type of friend she chooses. Of course I'm sure they look after her.'

'And we do have to keep in with them,' the Major reminded her. 'I need George!'

'All the same!' said Mrs Oliphant, 'and by the way,

she's out again tonight.'

'You worry too much, my dear. It's not as if we don't know where she is,' he said.

~

'It's another brilliant night,' said Audrey in a whisper for which there seemed no reason, since they were on the rubbish tip and, according to Bernie, quite alone.

Bernie had driven as far as possible along the track into the tip and turned to face the direction from which they had come. 'I always do this,' he said, 'in case we have unexpected company and have to leave in a hurry.'

'I thought you said there was no-one here,' said Audrey.

'Trust your Uncle Bernie! Why should there be? Who would want to be in this evil-smelling place other than ourselves? But I guard against all possibilities. Doesn't that show in all my inventions? Right, then. Now, Oliver, you take S.N.I.F.F.'

'Don't you mean S.M.E.L.L.?' Oliver asked in confusion.

'Now, listen again: it's perfectly straightforward,' said Bernie. 'Forget W.H.I.F.F. Concentrate on S.N.I.F.F. and S.M.E.L.L. Is W.H.I.F.F. bothering you, perhaps?'

'Not exactly,' replied Oliver.

'W.H.I.F.F.'s got nothing to do with this: it's for safe travelling at night.'

'It's just S.N.I.F.F. and S.M.E.L.L.: I know that,' said Oliver.

'S.N.I.F.F. is for finding it,' Bernie went on, 'and S.M.E.L.L. is for pumping it out and liquefying it.'

'I understand,' Oliver assured him.

'Right then, Oliver; you take S.N.I.F.F.,' said Bernie, 'and I will carry the end of the pipe which is joined to S.M.E.L.L. I'll stay lower down until you've found somewhere promising with S.N.I.F.F.'

'What do we do?' Audrey asked.

'Like I showed you. Prod it in the likely places until you get a good reading,' he said. 'Going uphill is hard work, with all that pipe behind me. Imagine what it's been like for me until now, carrying the pipe up on one arm, and sniffing with the other.'

'Surely you can't say "sniffing" like that?' said Audrey.

'In that sense, of course you can,' he replied. 'This should do it,' he said finally. Higher up, the mounds of old rubbish heaps rose out of the mist.

'Fine,' said Audrey. 'Come on, Olly!'

'Whistle until I can see where you are,' Bernie directed.

Later she said: 'I do wish he'd think of better names. If anybody heard us talk like this!'

'Well, they won't, will they?' Oliver grinned.

~

They quickly became lost in the shadows. Once or twice Audrey thought she saw a movement on the glistening slopes.

Then there were three more whistles, one after the other.

'But they're from different places,' Oliver said, his voice sounding flat with fear.

Then figures stalked out of the shadows into the moonlight, moving towards the car. She saw one stumble and go crashing down a slope into the mist.

Someone called out: 'There he is! After him!'

A moment later, Bernie was shouting at the top of his voice: 'Run for it! Take S.N.I.F.F.!'

'Follow me,' said Oliver. 'No matter what the ditches are like, it's our only chance.'

The shouts of the searchers grew distant. Audrey and Oliver clambered out of the mist. Ahead of them the ground had levelled.

'We're out of the tip,' said Oliver. 'Take a turn carrying S.N.I.F.F. I'm exhausted!'

Audrey asked in a small voice: 'What do you think is going to happen to Uncle Bernie?'

'I don't know. Nothing much, I should think.'

She shivered. In front of them, over a field, was the road to Ossington Cross.

They parted by Audrey's home. One or two people, made curious by the strong smell, had held up their lanterns, but the young people had passed unrecognised.

'I will ask Mary to take care of S.N.I.F.F.,' Audrey said, adding: 'Look, Oliver, you should not have been asked to help.'

He shrugged. 'I don't know why not,' he said.

'Good luck, Olly!'

~

When Audrey came into the kitchen she said simply: 'Mary, will you take this and put it somewhere safe? They've got Uncle Bernie at the tip.'

'Get your clothes off quick and wash down in the yard,' said Mary, without asking questions.

She put S.N.I.F.F. in the broom cupboard and said, 'That will do for the present. Lucky there's hot water on the stove. Wash all over and I'll get your night-dress and dressing gown.'

What seemed ages later, Mary was bringing hot milk to Audrey in bed. She said: 'I thought it would come to this. I hoped that it wouldn't. But there ...'

Mrs Oliphant came to the door, and standing there for a moment, had looked lonely and uncertain. Audrey longed to unburden herself, yet knew that she could not.

'Oh, so there you are, Mary. Some more candles are needed in the corridors. And Audrey, I do wish you'd have the kindness to call in and say goodnight when you return from the Inkpins. For all I know, you could have been out half the night. I have enough to worry about as it is.'

9

Caught!

It was bad enough: the anxiety about Bernie. The idea that something else was wrong occurred to Audrey while she was having breakfast.

Mary looked grim; not bothering even to say 'Anything else?'.

The Major had not said a word. He seemed to be wholly involved with his food. 'I'll be going now,' said Audrey.

'No,' said the Major.

Mary had come in again, but Mrs Oliphant, her eyes brimming with tears, waved her away.

'I'm sorry, Dad ... and Mum,' Audrey was admitting carefully. 'Yes I had tea at Uncle Bernie's. But how else could I see him? He hardly ever comes here, and he is my uncle!'

'We said don't see quite so much of him, that was all. It's his influence; with his general looks and untidiness and his hare-brained schemes. Well, everything! And

I'm sure he goes to that dreadful Fellini's,' said Mrs Oliphant.

'But you didn't really want me to see him and how could I tell him such a thing? So I've lied to him, too,' she said wretchedly.

'Well, if he doesn't know of our wishes he certainly shall,' said the Major. 'And if your mother had not called upon Mrs Inkpin last night ...'

' "They're having tea at Mr Weismann's!" That's what she told me!' said her mother.

'And rather a long tea!' said the Major. 'Why back so late?'

'But I asked if I could stay for supper,' Audrey said dully.

'All right. What could you have found to do at Bernie's all that time? Sit and talk? What about spending more time with your mother and father?'

Mrs Oliphant said, 'I asked Mary. Oh, we're not stupid, Audrey. She knows something, I'm sure.'

'What were you doing at Bernie's?' repeated the Major.

'Dad, what's wrong with Uncle Bernie?'

'We're discussing what's wrong with you: why you lied to us.'

'Mary won't say anything,' said Mrs Oliphant.

'And we can deal with her. How do we deal with you, Audrey?'

'I don't know, Dad.'

'I shall go and see Bernie,' said the Major.

'Please don't, Dad! In any case,' she faltered, 'he may not be there.'

But the Major stormed out.

~

Before leaving for Bernie's, he visited the kitchen.

'Well, Mary, no more nonsense!'

'What do you mean?'

'This: Have you been encouraging Audrey?'

'I would hope so. She needs encouragement.'

'You know very well what I mean; saying she was having tea at Mrs Inkpins.'

He walked up and down, clearing his throat, then stopped under one of the sides of smoked bacon which hung from the ceiling rafters.

'Thought there were four.'

'So there were. Missus said one stank, so I got rid of it.'

'Mary, I don't like your tone,' he said after a pause. 'You'd best leave at the end of the month.'

'Just as you wish,' she said.

~

When the Major reached Bernie's, his path was blocked by a policeman.

'What's this?' he asked.

'What's your business here, sir?' was the reply.

'What do you mean? Don't you know who I am?'

'Do you have anything to do with this house, then, sir?'

'I own it; as good as, anyway.'

The policeman glanced at a forlorn-looking individual at his side.

'Is this the one?'

'How could I say? I don't know,' the unhappy-looking man said, 'It was only the name I heard. I saw no-one. I said as much.'

'Your movements last night, sir.'

'What the devil do you mean?'

'Are you Sniff?' persisted the policeman.

'Am I Sniff? Who's Sniff?'

'We're trying to find out.'

'He called out: "Run for it; take Sniff!" ' said the forlorn man.

'Who did?' asked Major Oliphant. 'And who are you?'

'He helped arrest Mr Weismann at the tip, sir,' said the policeman.

'Look, I'm Oliphant,' said the Major, beginning to paw the ground.

'Oliphants' shoes!' said the forlorn-looking man, beginning to smile. 'Well I never; I've not had the pleasure ...'

'Weisman is my brother-in-law,' said the Major, clearing his throat. 'Is he in some sort of trouble?'

~

'The position, my dear,' he said later to his wife, 'is that Bernie has broken the law. Seen with his car on the Ossington tip.'

'You said the Ossington tip? Whatever for? And how did he manage it? Oh, that brother of mine!'

'They thought I was one of his accomplices. Someone called Sniff.'

'Who's he?'

'How should I know, Priscilla? Look, are you really asking me that?' he said irritably. 'All I know is we have the police at my brother-in-law's. Just what is the man up to?'

'Did you speak to him?'

'I said, "What's all this, Bernie?", and I got nothing back. No answers. Just sat there with that ridiculous large head of his resting in his hands.'

'Everything else he can help, but not his body.'

'And that fellow,' muttered the Major. 'Foul teeth, dirty neck. Leader of the people who trapped him. Not the police. It was a citizen's arrest.'

'It can't be done.'

'Oh yes it can! I could arrest Bessie Ottershaw for having my welly trimming knife in her shed.'

'That's ridiculous, Henry, and you know it.'

'Just making a point,' he said miserably. 'Now the police are interested. They might even take him in for questioning.'

And did Audrey know what was going on at the time, he wondered? Was she back at the house when it happened? It was just one thing after the other!

'And Mary tells me she's leaving,' said Mrs Oliphant. 'Who's going to take her place?'

'We've got to do something,' he replied, avoiding her question, 'and stand up to them. Not just Mary. All of them. I had a sergeant-major once. Came into my office, and said, "How's tricks?" Put him on a charge.'

'This is not the army.'

'What I'm trying to say is there's no respect. All over the place. Saw a notice outside Fellini's. *Socks dried*. No respect for the food regulations. Bernie gets liquefied gas from somewhere; must have; apparently no bag seen on top of his car; quite illegal; then drives around a rubbish tip. I ask you. No respect for the law. Mary talks to me in an off-hand way. Comes up to the table and says "Anything else?" in that way of hers. Bit like "How's tricks?" D'you think she's ever heard of "Is everything all right, sir? madam?" And it's the tone, Priscilla. It's how she says it.'

'I've often pointed it out.'

'No respect for me.'

'Do you expect me to do the cooking and cleaning?' she asked after a pause.

'We'll find somebody.'

'You could have left it just now,' she said. 'Now, of all times!

'I must admit,' he said wearily, 'normally I wouldn't have done it. It's your brother! The whole affair has affected my judgement.'

'I do understand,' said Mrs Oliphant, 'but please make sure she does not go until we have found someone else.'

~

'Mary, I do not wish to be hard on you. Neither, I might add, does Mrs Oliphant.'

'Fancy that,' she said.

'There is no hurry for you to leave.'

'Just a minute,' she said going to the back door in answer to a sustained knocking.

'No, I do not!' came her voice. Then: 'You'll not have it!'

The Major had risen to satisfy his curiosity and then seen the forlorn face of the man with the dirty teeth: the same man who had arrested Bernie! Seeing the Major, the forlorn man broke into a smile, saying, 'Well, I never!'

'Out you go,' said Mary, pushing him.

'Who was that?' the Major asked carelessly.

'My cousin, more's the pity.'

'And what, if it is not an impolite question,' he asked looking as if he was just about to read the lesson in church, having first obtained the attention of all the people, the fidgeting choir-boys, and the mice as well, 'did your wholly admirable cousin want?'

'Some ham,' said Mary.

'Next time you see him, give him some: lots of it,' he replied, thinking fast. 'And Mary, not only is there no hurry about going, we would on reflection like you to stay.'

'Suit yourself,' she said. 'Now I'd best get on.'

~

'When things happen like this, it makes me think it's all for nothing. All the effort. The sorting it out in your mind. Cleaning teeth. Moustache. Everything. What for? Taking another biscuit. Making way for an old lady. Anything you care to mention. Opening a new welly shop.'

'Henry, do stop it! What are you talking about?'

'Living.'

'What about it?'

'When our own servant's relation has made a citizen's arrest of your brother, Priscilla, then it makes me think it's all for nothing.'

'I do understand. I'm beginning to think it is a faulty gene of the Weismanns.'

'Do not talk nonsense, Priscilla. You're not suggesting

that you, too, have the desire to potter around on the Ossington municipal tip?'

'I should hope not,' she smiled through forming tears.

'To think,' he went on,' that I have had to offer her the job back. How can we do otherwise? We dare not make an enemy of this wretched man, or of Mary.'

'Will it go to court, dear?'

'If it does, at least that dirty-looking ruffian may be persuaded not to mention our family connection, nor to ruin our reputations for as long as he eats ham and Mary is there to give it to him.'

'Ham?'

'Ham, dear, ham,' he said irritably. 'And d'you know all she said after I'd offered her the job back? "Suit yourself." Just like that! I can put up with one or two people like Bessie Ottershaw, staring daggers at me. Looking at me, disregarding my nod. Nostrils as rigid as a tent that's just been put up. Flapping a bit. And Mary! Now we're told she's related to that wretched man! But I will put up with it, Priscilla. For the good of my name, I will put up with it.'

The Major wandered up and down the corridors of his home several times, gazing at portraits of his ancestors, muttering *Olifans vincit omnia*. Over the next few days he took to doing it regularly, in the late afternoon just after Mary had lit the candles. Sometimes just before. He had heard no further news of Bernie, except that he was due to appear in court on a charge of illegal travel.

~

He noticed that Audrey was looking pale and drawn, and decided not to question her further at present. At least, he thought, she was keeping indoors in the evenings as he had ordered; while the shadows bounced about, and the candle-light gleamed in her hair: already she was looking as if one day she'd be quite as beautiful as some of the Oliphant ladies in the corridor.

10

Bernie on Trial

It was the day on which Bernie Weismann was due to appear in court charged with an offence under the Travel Act. Breakfast had been difficult. When Mary brought in the cold sausage, Audrey simply said: 'I can't!'

Mrs Oliphant had made-up with extra care, but Audrey knew very well that she'd been crying.

'Couldn't you go too, Dad?' she asked, longing for a united family on this day, most of all.

'No,' said the Major, 'I've hired the town hall; I'm giving a lecture there, this afternoon.'

'What is it about, Dad? Couldn't it wait?'

'I'm calling it: The Thing To Do. And no, it can't wait,' he replied.

'It's bound to be about wellies,' said her mother bitterly.

'Yes, wellies,' he snapped. 'I do not wish to think about what is happening today. And there's nothing, I suppose,' he continued, as he toyed with a piece of marmalade peel which reminded him of a chunk of recycled welly, although it was some time ago, at Liverpool, that he had seen such a thing '... nothing that I can say that will persuade you not to go?'

'I think we have discussed it.'

'People will connect us. Of course George knows; the vicar, too. But now everyone will know!'

'But we are connected, Henry. He's my brother.'

'Mum, you're going because Uncle Bernie's your brother,' said Audrey.

'No matter what!' She added: 'I'm truly sorry you're not coming, Henry.'

'And he's my uncle; I'd like to go too,' said Audrey.

Mary, who had stopped as if to look at the polish on the sideboard, left for the kitchen with a smile and a nod of approval as Mrs Oliphant said, 'Very well, Audrey. Go and change into something more suitable. We do not want to let your Uncle Bernie down.'

~

The jurors fidgeted because of the serious nature of the charge facing the man in the dock. The court room was stuffy and a fat juror had taken off his shoes for an airing. This added to the stuffiness. Several more jurors having seen this, slyly followed suit without being noticed by the court.

The forlorn man with the bad teeth had been called to the witness box.

'That's him,' he said, nodding at Bernie.

'Did you see Sniff?' asked the counsel for the defence.

'I did not; I keep on saying I didn't.'

'Just answer the question,' said the judge, who was

known for his irritability.

'The defendant, is, you will have heard, an inventor,' Bernie's counsel said. 'He has invented something he calls a S.M.E.L.L., although because he wishes to keep them secret we are not privileged to know what these letters stand for. Now has it not occurred to you, members of the jury, that Sniff stands for a thing, and is, in fact, S.N.I.F.F.? "Run for it ... take Sniff!" What was Sniff doing on Ossington tip, if he needed to be "taken"? Had he injured a leg? There may indeed have been one accomplice, or even more: my client will not say; but S.N.I.F.F. was not one of them! S.N.I.F.F. is indeed a thing.'

'What, then, does S.N.I.F.F. stand for,' interrupted the judge, 'if that is the case?'

'My client will not answer, at least not sensibly, your honour, and has not done so in court.'

'How, then, did he answer you, in or out of court, privately or not? If you know, you must tell the court.'

'He is under some strain, your honour,' said the defence counsel awkwardly. 'He feels his inventions ... that the charges brought against him, do not take account of the great benefits he offers to mankind.'

'How did he answer?' snapped the judge, whose name was Fanshaw.

'Say Nothing In Front of Fanshaw,' whispered the defence, a young man who had not yet learned that forgetfulness could on occasions be useful.

There was some laughter in court and the judge turned the rather rich white of a plucked free-range chicken.

Nor had the prisoner's performance in the witness

box improved the judge's impression. Bernie would not
answer the prosecution; he would not say what
S.N.I.F.F. did, or where it might be, or who his accomplices were; although he did say, quite clearly, as his
glance swept the packed court, 'I would not in any
circumstances declare the identity of those who helped,
nor would I want those responsible to admit it. It is the
last thing I would want.'

On hearing this, Audrey had started to tremble with
emotion. 'He's not helping himself,' she whispered.

~

'It is not your duty,' the judge was saying in his sum-
ming-up, 'to decide the value of these inventions. I find
anything named S.M.E.L.L. or S.N.I.F.F. suspicious. It
does little for the defendant's character that he has given
them such names. What sort of man, you may ask, calls
anything a S.M.E.L.L.? And he has admitted that a
further device exists about which little is known except
that it is called a W.H.I.F.F. When questioned by the
police, he was, in a moment of forgetfulness perhaps,
kind enough to state that a device on the front of his car,
which is to do in some way with this W.H.I.F.F., was,
members of the jury, a frog scooper. Several people
whose common sense may be relied upon have said that
this device, which they have examined, does indeed
smell of frogs.

'He has refused to tell the court what was his purpose
on the Ossington municipal tip, or what any of the
names stand for. He has been foolish enough to say
what S.N.I.F.F. might have stood for, and had he poked
fun at the bench in court and had it not simply been

repeated by his unfortunate counsel, I would have sent him down for contempt. The defendant's learned counsel might well have entered a plea of insanity, but he has not done so, perhaps mistakenly, and you will not therefore take into account that possibility.

'It is your duty to decide whether, when he travelled the road to reach the Ossington tip he did or did not break the law, which states that all travel, other than by foot ...'

'What if you've got leaky wellies?' called out a voice in the gallery, followed by a scuffle.

'Other than by foot,' repeated the judge, 'horse and cart, or bicycle if you are fortunate enough to have tyres for it,' he added to avoid further interruptions, 'is forbidden.' Such actions as the defendant is accused of threaten the security of the state. Only emergency services may use ordinary methane gas. If everyone did, the crops would vanish; we would soon have little to eat. Only the government cars may use liquefied gas, the dwindling supplies of which are for them and them alone, and for the grid and the completion of our nuclear fusion programme, which one day will fill the grid with its own power.

'The defendant claims that he is able to liquefy the gas on the tips. You have heard that no means is known of doing this on a small scale. He will not tell us what his so-called invention stands for. Members of the jury, it is your duty to consider whether anything,' and here the judge paused and looked severely at Bernie, 'he or his counsel have said, should be taken seriously into account.'

The court reassembled after lunch. The jury returned

their verdict and the judge, with great contentment, pronounced sentence of three months.

Before being led away, Bernie, pale and drawn, gazed for an instant towards Mrs Oliphant and Audrey. A voice cried out from the gallery: 'The court's a fool!' and an outraged face, very much like Mary's, appeared and disappeared again in the general crush. The fat juror tripped headlong over his undone shoes laces and there were various cries of 'Arrest that woman!' 'Fanshaw's a menace!' 'Clear the court!'

Mrs Oliphant was saying, 'Bernie, how could you do this!'

Audrey, her own eyes filled with tears, cried out, 'What will happen to him? Poor Uncle Bernie!' In the corridors she was hit in the back with someone's brief-case. Everyone seemed to be talking at once; half of them anxious to leave the building and the other half, by not moving, stopping them from doing so. The for-lorn-looking man, who wanted to avoid Mary, was pressed in a corner, picking his teeth.

Out in the open, Audrey said: ' Mum, what about Cherry? I've just got to look after her.'

'Cherry?'

'Uncle Bernie's dog.'

Mrs Oliphant shrugged, saying, 'Yes, of course ... the dog.'

'All right, Mum?'

'I wish your father had been here,' she said, rather to herself than to Audrey.

Then it was all over. And in the streets there were familiar sounds: of horses and carts; the roar of one of the winds which sprang up so quickly, tearing tufts of

leaves from the town trees, then dying back; house
doors shutting; people walking and talking, crying out;
insults, greetings, questions. A solemn hum of noise
came through the opened street door of Fellini's, and
with it the smell of cooking.

Audrey thought: everything is the same as it was, for
all of us.

But not for Bernie.

~

'It didn't go well,' said the Major gloomily. 'Hardly
anyone there. Perhaps the title: "The Thing To Do", is
not a good one for a lecture?'

'It doesn't tell people what to expect, Henry,' she said
wearily, having just returned from court.

' "What Thing", I expected people to ask. Followed
by: "To Do What?" and I would have told 'em! Let's
have your old wellies! Thought it would persuade people
to part with them. Also spoke about the wretchedness
of wet feet.'

'Bernie got three months.' Mrs Oliphant said.

After a pause he asked: 'Where's Audrey?'

'At Bernie's, feeding the dog.'

'Look, Priscilla, you mustn't think I don't care: I do.
Just using wellies to blot out things that worry me.'

'Try your wellies on this, then,' she said grimly.
'Audrey was there, on the tip. I've had my suspicions:
after watching her in court, I'm sure.'

11

More Complications for Audrey

'Yes, I was there and so was Oliver ... we just had to help Uncle Bernie. Dad ... Mum, look, I'm really sorry I didn't tell you, but you would only have stopped us.'

'It would have been better for you if we had,' her mother said.

'Perhaps so,' Audrey managed to whisper.

'Before we were obliged to send you to the local school because of the Collapse, we sent you to St Cuthbert's,' her father began. 'It cost a great deal of money. It took the profit on just about 1,200 pairs of wellies per term.

'People work hard. They worry. I used to worry about the day's production even when I was eating breakfast. Salesmen going into welly shops would worry; will Mrs Cleghorn buy or not, depending on her corns? Should he ask how they were?'

'If you were brief and to the point, Henry, we might persuade Audrey ...'

'Yes, I could be brief, but it would not benefit Audrey.'

'I am truly sorry, Dad.'

Here the Major fell silent. He looked haggard.

'You can see how you've upset your father!'

'Our maid's relation has brought us low. We are obliged to give him ham to keep him as quiet as possible at the trial, so that our good name is not dragged into it: but now I find that because you, as well as Bernie, were breaking the law ... it will be, anyway.'

'Dad, it seemed the right thing to do!'

'No-one need know, Henry,' said Mrs Oliphant.

'I'm afraid so: it's illegal, can't you understand?' he said.

'Please, Dad ...'

'I have never,' said the Major, spinning round to face Audrey, 'had anything but the greatest admiration for the police. You will come with me later this afternoon to the police station, and you will take your medicine, my girl. I do not shirk my responsibilities.'

'Now, Audrey, see what you've done!' said Mrs Oliphant.

'Yes, I wanted to keep it dark,' cried the Major. 'Give him, that wretched fellow, a little ham. Hurt my pride. But this, Audrey, has gone too far. A visit to the police station will do more for you in the way of character building than St Cuthbert's ever did.'

Audrey had rushed from the room. Her pillow was damp with tears. Lying there, waiting, she thought: So, my pillow's damp. Everything's damp. Oh, I wish I was miles from here!

~

The house seemed even quieter than usual. Mary had gone into town to buy some bread. The Major was alone in his study, still determined to see the police, but dreading it all the same. He was biting his knuckles. Suddenly he exploded: 'Blast Bernie Weismann! Blast him off the face of the earth!'

He wanted a cup of herb tea. He rang for Mary. Finally he went down to the kitchen to get it himself. There were sounds from there. He was just about to say, 'Didn't you hear me, Mary?' when he saw the forlorn-looking man quickly moving to the back door, clutching a cold leg of lamb.

'Hey, you!' said the Major.

'I was looking for Mary.'

'What have you got?'

The forlorn man tried to manage a smile, but shrugged instead.

'Meat.' The Major turned purple. 'My meat.'

'Mary said you'd said, if I wanted a little ham ...'

'Not ham. Huge leg of lamb. Worth a welly at least. Give it back. And I'm telling the police everything, so you can't blackmail me any more, all right? Now get out! And consider yourself lucky I'm not reporting you. Understand?'

'Perfectly,' said the forlorn man, sounding matter of fact. 'Couldn't see any ham, although I looked everywhere. No ham in the pantry, no ham in the 'fridge; although it wouldn't be switched on, anyway, would it?'

'I suppose not,' muttered the Major, not feeling inclined to have a conversation. 'Now, off you go!'

'No ham in the broom cupboard, even.'

'In the broom cupboard? ' asked the Major, in spite of himself.

'Just looking,' said the man.

'Right,' said the Major, coming to, 'now out you get!'

'But there was something else in there,' the forlorn man replied. 'To me, putting two and two together, it looks as if it's S.N.I.F.F. You know, S.N.I.F.F., they've been looking for.'

'Sniff? In there: poor fellow?' said the Major weakly. 'Who's Sniff?

~

Mrs Oliphant and Audrey had been summoned. Mrs Oliphant was leaning back on the kitchen dresser for support. The forlorn man was seated alone at the kitchen table saying to a grim-faced Mary, back from the bakers, 'I'll have another spoonful of sugar.'

'You'll do without,' said Mary.

But the Major said: 'No he won't. Fetch the sugar bowl, Audrey, and then perhaps someone will now be good enough to tell me why this is in the cupboard.'

'I brought it home, Dad; what else could I do?'

'And there wasn't anywhere else to put it,' said Mary.

'And exactly what is it?' asked the Major quietly. 'Priscilla, since you attended court, perhaps you will tell me? Did Bernie say what it stood for?'

'Say Nothing In Front of Fanshaw,' said Mrs Oliphant, pulling out her handkerchief.

'It seems, doesn't it, Audrey, that the entire family is now involved. Your mother, as you can see, has been reduced to a pitiable state.'

Without looking up, and biting her lip, Audrey said: 'Hiding it seemed the best thing to do at the time.'

'Of course, I am not involved, nor is your mother. But it looks as if we are, thanks entirely to you.'

'You can rest assured,' said Mary's cousin, gripping the bony end of the leg of lamb with meaning, 'that they shall not hear a word of it from my lips.'

'And I am sure, Henry, quite sure that you should now let the whole matter drop; you should not go to the police about Audrey's role in this dismal affair. It cannot help Bernie. And, what's more, it wouldn't help us. Think of your reputation, Henry!'

'Since it is your wish, then I will drop the matter, my dear,' said the Major immediately. 'But I shall have more to say to you, Audrey.'

'In the meantime, I'd best be getting along,' said the forlorn man.

'One minute!' called the Major. 'Mary; some pickle. Dear fellow, would you like a pot of pickle to go with it?'

~

The forlorn man had gone, but they were all still in the kitchen. The Major could not let things rest. 'Before you go to your room, Audrey, I wish you to answer me this question. Clearly your mother has the wrong end of the stick. I did not intend to pursue the question in front of that ... in front of Mary's cousin.'

'Call him what you will,' Mary said.

'Yes, well, that wretched fellow. Now, what I want to know,' he continued, 'is who's Fanshaw, I mean, it is a name, isn't it? It's not F.A.N.S.H.A.W., one of those wretched things like S.N.I.F.F.?'

'Fanshaw's the judge, Dad. It was just Uncle Bernie ...'

'What does it mean, then?'

'A Secret and Neat Invention for Finding Foulness.'

'I do not feel in the mood for playing games,' warned the Major. 'Fanshaw doesn't come into it?'

'That's right.'

'Very well, what does it do?'

'It finds where there are pockets of methane gas. In places like rubbish tips.'

'Then what?'

'Then you screw in S.M.E.L.L.s nozzle.'

'Which stands for?'

'Stinky Methane Extractor Liquefier and Lozenger.'

'It can actually turn gas into lozenges? That's quite remarkably handy.'

'I've always told you, he's a genius, your Uncle Bernie,' said Mary.

'That will do!' said Mrs Oliphant.

'It's the only bit of it that isn't true,' admitted Audrey.

'Then why?'

'Because SMELL has two L's. He had to find a reason for the other L.'

'Yes, I see. The whole thing's remarkable, Priscilla. If he had gone about it another way.'

'But he broke the law,' said Mrs Oliphant.

'Yes,' said the Major, 'he broke the law. He asked two children to help him do so, in that rat-infested rubbish tip.'

'Dad, you won't tell the police about me?'

'Not now,' the Major coughed. 'Not, er ... in everybody's interest.'

'There's the problem of Cherry,' said Mrs Oliphant.

'Mary, you'll go to Mr Weismann's and feed the dog until we can find another home for it,' said the Major.

'Dad, can I go too?'

'You may help Mary with the dog. But I forbid you absolutely to set foot in that house after your uncle's return. You will then be banned from going there. Do I make myself clear?'

'Pretty clear, yes.'

'Come, Mary, help me to hide S.N.I.F.F. in the cellar.'

'It's simply not fair, Dad,' Audrey added.

Receiving no reply she said no more, realising that it would be useless to do so at the present time.

12

A Visit to Prison

'Let me come with you to the prison!' Audrey pleaded.

'It's deceiving your parents again,' said Mary.

'Dad will change his mind.'

'But right now, he means it sure enough!'

'Yes, but he didn't actually say I couldn't visit him in prison.'

'I'm sure it never crossed his mind that you would want to. And in any case he must know that children under sixteen aren't allowed into prison anyway, unless they're with an adult.'

'But you're going to see him?' Audrey persisted.

'Of course I am. He'll be worried about his plants and things. And I could take him some sandwiches.'

'They probably don't allow it,' Audrey said.

'It's a tragedy, that's what it is. Such a kind and brilliant man.'

'Mary, no one need know. And I think he'd like to see me.'

'Yes, he would.' She paused. 'Very well, but I only

hope you know what you're doing,' adding, '... and that applies to me too, for that matter.'

~

They sat facing Bernie, watched by the warder.

'This is no place for you,' said Bernie at last, 'although I'm glad you're here.' Taking her hand in his, he added, 'What ever made me do it, Audrey?'

'I think it's all amazing, really. So do Oliver and Mary. Most people would, if they knew what you were really doing. So would Dad, he really would, if you'd only listen to each other. And as for W.H.I.F.F.!' Audrey's eyes were bright and her face was flushed.

'What I meant was,' said Bernie gently, 'I should not have asked you and Oliver to help.'

'The only danger was the rats, and there's Cherry. You said yourself that with Cherry ...'

'Yes, and I was going to ask you, who's looking after her?'

'We are, aren't we, Mary?'

'I broke the law, Audrey,' said Bernie after a pause, 'and it's just good luck that you haven't a criminal record because of me.'

'Well, I haven't got one, so don't worry about it,' replied Audrey. 'And we're going straight to your home after we leave here. Oliver will be there, and the three of us will do everything that's needed.'

'I've been feeding the dog these last two days,' Mary said, then she was soon telling him about S.N.I.F.F. and how that morning she and the Major had hidden it in the cellar.

'I wish Priscilla could visit me, but then I dare say

Henry would not like it.'

'If they do come to see you, Mr Weismann,' said Mary, 'it would be as well not to mention this visit.'

'Why not?' asked Bernie.

'They've forbidden Audrey to see you. It's best to come out with it.'

'Uncle, it's so unreasonable!'

Bernie remained silent, his shoulders looking more rounded than ever.

'Then,' said Bernie at last, 'you must obey your father. Perhaps, Audrey, my dear, one day he will change his mind.'

'Uncle Bernie! ...'

'There is one thing I would ask you to do for me. Go to Fellini's.'

Bernie had risen to his feet and nodded to the warder.

'I'll go for you. I'll gladly go to Fellini's,' said Audrey, in a barely audible voice. 'What is it?'

'It's my socks, Angel; he has some socks of mine, and I do not have the ticket. The prison warders took the ticket; it's number 72. They also took my watch and keys ...'

'Mr Fellini has your socks?' asked Audrey.

'I had to hand in this ticket. Just tell Mr Fellini the number. He's got two pairs of socks, and if they're not collected, he charges.'

With that, he turned back to the cells.

~

Oliver was gazing at Bernie's car when Mary and Audrey arrived.

'Cherry's sitting by the back door,' he said. 'How was Bernie?'

'As well as you'd expect,' said Mary. 'And when did they return the car?' She bent down over the frog scooper, adding: 'It's a marvel there are no frog parts at all. No legs or anything. The police may have cleaned it, of course.'

'If Uncle said they were scooped up, then I'm sure they wouldn't have been hurt. I'm sure of it: he's like that,' said Audrey firmly.

'That is so,' said Mary, getting on her knees to smell it. 'And I don't have to be an expert to say it smells of frogs.'

By now, Cherry had joined them.

'Come on, you poor old girl,' said Audrey.

Oliver asked: 'Did Bernie say much?'

'No, not much,' Audrey replied.

He noticed her swollen eyelids and said no more.

It was Oliver who saw the notebook on the kitchen dresser and as a consequence said something he immediately regretted. It was propped up near a dinner plate. Bernie had drawn a good likeness of a frog on the front cover and underneath it had written: F.R.Y.I.N.G. TIMES.

'Are you sure about what you just said? The frogs, I mean,' he said. 'My grandpa remembers eating sparrow dumpling, as a child.'

'That sort of thing's coming back,' said Mary, who was polishing some brass and was unaware of where the conversation was heading. 'Sparrow dumplings, yes, and things like that. Why not? People had nearly forgotten about good wholesome food. Pigeon pie, stewed rabbit: beautiful!'

'It's got all the times,' said Oliver, turning the pages.

'Masses of them. He's numbered them all. Look!'

Audrey had taken the book.

'The average F.R.Y.I.N.G. TIME,' she read out, as Mary straightened up and looked at her puckered face with concern, 'on 149 frogs was therefore eleven minutes and twenty-two seconds. I don't believe it,' said Audrey brokenly.

'Give it here,' said Mary. She glanced through it several times. 'Well, if your uncle did have his little weaknesses, it's not right for us to be prying into them with him not being here to speak for himself.'

'He never would do it. He told me what the scooper was for, and I believe him.'

'It does seem an extraordinary thing: to keep a record of how long it takes,' said Mary.

'Perhaps he was going to write a cookery book one day,' Oliver suggested.

'He wouldn't have anything to do with it. You don't understand Uncle Bernie.'

'It would only be for the legs, of course,' said Mary. 'But eleven minutes, coming on for twelve! They'd be burned to a frazzle.'

'But look,' said Oliver, 'it's not FRYING TIMES. It's F.R.Y.I.N.G. TIMES.'

'So it is,' Mary said, looking at the back again. 'Audrey, you've more sense than any of us. Look at it, here it is, "Frog Recovery From Yawning in Nearby Ground times". Except that on no account do frogs yawn.'

'Of course they don't,' Audrey said. 'It's the same as lozenges. It's the only thing he's not always accurate with.'

'I daresay he means the frogs being insensible,' said Mary. 'Knocked off their feet at great speed and recovering in the roadside ditches after they've been scooped.'

'Why would he want to know a thing like that?' asked Oliver. 'To have gone to all that trouble, and the testing ...'

'Because he would not wish to hurt them seriously, just as he explained,' said Audrey, smiling for the first time that day, 'and probably he wanted to know what speed he could safely travel at, for the frogs, I mean, when scooping.'

After giving Cherry some food, Mary said, 'Don't forget Fellini's. Then we'd best return home.'

They put fresh blankets in Cherry's basket which was in the back door porch, away from the dampness.

'I don't know what's going to happen to her,' said Mary, as they started walking along the Ossington Road and into town.

'We could have her, if your parents won't,' said Oliver.

'She'll never leave, my dear. I reckon she'll be there until the day he returns,' Mary replied.

~

Inside Fellini's, even during the day, it was difficult to see because of the blinding sunlight which streamed in from the opened front door, and the contrasting shadows which swallowed the tables and the late diners. A waiter was going round the tables scraping off the fallen candle wax from the night before.

As they waited, Audrey noticed that one old gentleman was bare footed. As her eyes became accustomed to the light she could see two other pairs of white feet gradually take shape in the distance.

'We don't want to eat,' said Mary, 'we've come to collect Mr Weismann's socks; ticket number 72, only we don't have the ticket.'

'We're not allowed to give socks without we get no ticket,' said the waiter.

'Look, we don't want trouble,' said Mary firmly. 'His socks please!'

Meanwhile Mr Fellini had come to their table. 'You say Mr Weismann? Are you friends of his?'

'He's my uncle,' said Audrey.

'You mind if I sit with you? For a long time Bernie comes here. I never know he's connected with Oliphanti Shoes until the court case. Oliphanti is a great man. I go to his lecture, but only two, maybe three other people are there. Such a pity for it is good sense, all this dry feet business. I go because of what he call it!'

' "The Thing To Do",' said Audrey.

'That's right! What thing? I ask. What to do? I ask.'

'He'd be very pleased to hear you say that,' said Audrey, biting her lip. 'He's had so much to disappoint him lately.'

'And fancy Bernie having such famous relations! I am very sad to hear he's gone to prison. When he comes out, I am interested in this frog scooper. The legs, with a little garlic and butter ...' Here Mr Fellini pressed his fingers to his lips.

'It's not like that at all, Mr Fellini. If we could just have his socks.'

'Of course, Miss Oliphanti,' he beamed. 'I never before

speak to an Oliphanti. Perhaps you tell your father, that I too, Eduardo Fellini, also believe in dry feet. And if Bernie don't go to prison for having trouble with his sniff ...'

'It's really a S.N.I.F.F.' said Audrey.

'I say a sniff. Without this sniff, I don't get a chance to speak to an Oliphanti!'

~

The Major had asked Audrey about S.M.E.L.L. 'You screw in the nozzle and then what?'

She repeated what she knew, and he then lapsed into a silence.

Sighing, she thought: if only you and Uncle Bernie at least had something in common. What she did not and could not know, was that it was to be her father's interest in wellingtons which, in fact, would bring this about.

13

All for Wellies

Although the Major's lecture entitled: The Thing To Do had not been a success, his door-to-door calling had. The people from the town and the surrounding villages handed over most of their old wellies. He gave certificates promising them a five per cent discount if they bought his new, recycled wellyphants, although no-one, of course, could say when that would be.

Obliging ladies found wellies in attics, in sheds. Old men appeared in the doorways, beckoning the Major in to unlit houses, to look under stairs. People with noses that stood out in the gloom, with their dogs capering about on the worn carpets in the shadows, searched everywhere. Some places like this did not even have candles ... and the strong kitchen smells!

There had been the stooped old gentleman at his kitchen table; spoon stuck into stiff jelly. The Major had said: 'Your wife tells me you have some old wellies in the shed.'

'Can't stop,' said the man. 'Lots to do.'

'Come on, Arthur!' said the lady.

'A five per cent off, on a future purchase,' said the Major, adding, under his breath, 'Long time in future.'

'Can't move about,' said the old man, trying to get his spoon out. 'My legs are like lead.'

'Want to recycle them,' said the Major.

'You should have mentioned that before,' said the old man, getting up. 'One minute,' he went on, watching the cream flow into the crack in the jelly.

'Pull yourself together, Arthur,' said the lady. 'These gentlemen haven't got all morning.'

But Bessie Ottershaw had hung on to her wellies. When the Major had knocked, he saw her face disappear over the geraniums in the window.

He scribbled a note: 'Want old wellies ... Oliphant.' and slid it under the door. A moment later the paper slid out signed B. Ottershaw, and a message reading: 'So do I ... new ones. Trimmed your wellies for nigh on twenty years!'

'Drat the woman!' he said to George. 'I know she's got some in the shed. Why doesn't she come to the door?'

'We've got most of them in,' said George, 'so why bother with Bessie?'

But the Major had finally got her to open the door.

'A five per cent discount ...' he began.

'I've heard about it. Not interested.'

Like the better class of brush salesmen, he put his foot in the door.

''Ere, d'you mind?'

Apart from people like her, it worked. It worked beautifully. And one day he would make a lot of money

just recycling the few wellies he had collected locally.
He had given a pair of new wellies from his precious
store to a man with horse and cart, who had dumped
the old wellies in the factory car park. It was easy.

But just think of the old wellies in other parts of the
country! There was a huge fortune out there, and he
could not get at it! Beyond the hills: there were other
towns, huddled here and there, black at night, no street
lights, no cars. People lolling in shop doorways. In cafés.
All of them, these towns, full of discarded wellingtons
that could be had for nothing.

What he wanted was more welly dumps, so that
when the new-age power was there, the dumps of wellies throughout the United Kingdom could be collected
and taken to Oliphant Footwear. But he could not travel
to start the dumps. It was a dream: it was illegal . . .
impossible! Bernie had travelled, and only to the
municipal tip and think of the trouble that had caused
him: three months in jail.

Bernie. Yes. Bernie and his car. A flash of inspiration
came into the Major's mind. Bernie's car! Everything
legal and above board and travelling around the country in Bernie's car, starting welly dumps!

He'd have to get Bernie out of jail: that was the first
step.

~

He decided to visit him.

'I may at times have been hard on you, Bernie. We've
had disagreements. But I want to help you.'

'Why are you here?'

'I told you, to see what I can do.'

'For yourself; not for me. You've never done anything
for me ... But no, that's not true. You lent me money for
the house.'

'Forget it. Money is not everything.'

'Now I know you're lying to me,' said Bernie.

'Do you want me to help, or not?' asked the Major,
flushing with annoyance.

'Very well, we wait and see why you do this. But, yes,
I want you to help. What are you going to do for me?'

'Pay for a good solicitor for a start. The one you had,'
the Major said, 'was to blame for such a sentence; letting
slip about Fanshaw.'

'You mean, appeal?'

'That's right. It was an outrageous sentence.'

'What is it: what do you want?' said Bernie after a
pause. 'And you better be quick about it: visiting time
is short.'

'I need your car to travel. Of course, first of all I'll get
permission.'

'Oh, so you will?' Bernie smiled.

'Yes, I have a friend in the government. If I can trace
him, it will all be above board and legal, and an addi-
tional source of liquefied gas will be of great interest to
them.'

'You wouldn't do it the way I did it?' asked Bernie.

'Take on the law? Certainly not! And there's bound
to be money in it for you if you go the right way about
it, but first of all we must get you out of here.'

'Then we can all be friends; you and I, and my sister.
And what about Audrey?'

'There's no problem,' said the Major, becoming wary
of Bernie's tone.

'And do you think it's good for Audrey, when one moment you say "Don't do this, don't see your Uncle Bernie" and then, "OK, see him"? And I know you do all this chopping and changing, just on account of wellingtons!'

'Who said it's for wellingtons?'

'With you, it has to be wellingtons.'

'Very well,' admitted the Major.

'Look,' said Bernie, 'just explain more fully: why do you need my car?'

'To travel throughout the UK and to start huge welly dumps, property of Oliphants Footwear. Reward people who organise each with a pair of wellies.'

'Then what?'

'Collect them by the lorry load when travel is possible again. Wham and there we are.'

'Wham?'

'Recycle. Earmuffs. And I'll make you a Director.'

'You can keep it,' said Bernie.

The warder looked at the clock.

'I'll get you out,' said the Major. 'What do you think?'

'Never once again do you put Audrey and her friends against me.'

'Never.'

'Just like that? But of course, like I said, you'll do anything for wellingtons.'

'Wellyphants.'

'I pretend not to hear this. But you don't ever drive my Bentley.'

'Very well; I don't see that it matters who drives. And I'm prepared to help you with your gas liquefier, and so on.'

'If you want to get anywhere, and I rather think you do, then you'll have to help. You have no choice!' said Bernie.

'You have to show me your equipment of course. S.N.I.F.F. and all that.'

'OK, you help with S.N.I.F.F.; I can't manage alone. But I'm the one who drives and you must sit in the back.'

~

After Sunday lunch the Major had suddenly suggested that he and Mrs Oliphant should go and visit Bernie in jail.

'Dear old Dad,' Audrey said, 'I knew he couldn't keep it up: I'm so happy, Mary!'

She replied: 'What your father's up to, I don't know. But it's something!'

Audrey waited: it was almost as if by patiently doing so, that something else was bound to happen.

During the week she went with Oliver to feed Cherry. The sweat rolled off her. From the direction of Ossington she smelled Mr Hood's pig farm. All week there had not been enough wind to flutter the leaves, only enough to bring this smell.

In the fields the horses worked, heads down, bodies rippling. Some were bringing in beet for the digesters; some cutting the crops of wheat.

One day, when she got home from Bernie's house, Mrs Oliphant asked: 'Have you seen your father? He's late for lunch.'

~

Exhausted and stumbling, the Major was dragging rusted oil drums out of a ditch. Soon, with the aid of some planks of wood he had erected a barricade.

At four o'clock he emerged from behind a bush. According to his observations, a government car was now due on one of its journeys. He mopped his face to stop the sweat running into his eyes and waited.

Soon there was the sound of screeching brakes. Two men leaped out, and grabbing the Major, bundled him into the car.

They had reversed into the shelter of a high bank.

'It's not an ambush, I tell you,' said the Major.

While the barricade was being dismantled by the two men who had seized him, an older man, who appeared to be an official of some importance, started to question him.

'I keep on telling you,' said the Major, 'I've an urgent matter to discuss. Something the government should know.'

'Just answer my question. Do you know it's an offence to stop a government car?'

'Yes, yes, I know. I wanted to get a message about all this to my friend Parker. He'd listen, but I don't know where he is. So I thought this barricade was the only way.'

'Parker?'

'Gordon Hiram Parker.'

'What, old Nosey Parker?'

'Good Lord, yes,' said the Major. 'You know him? That's splendid!'

'It helps,' admitted the other. 'Nevertheless, I've every right to arrest you. But I'd better listen.'

~

'And so you see, it's surely of importance to the government. And in the meantime he's in jail and only he can properly explain what it is all about.'

'We have our own limited supplies of liquid North-Sea gas, I can assure you,' said the official. 'If it is true that Mr Weismann can liquefy small quantities of gas, using another method, then I think we should know all about it. It could be strategically important to have other sources of gas for use in emergency.'

'Exactly!' said the Major. 'And, of course, my brother-in-law needs to travel all over the country to test his equipment, and to investigate as many rubbish tips as he can.'

'But naturally,' agreed the official.

'He will need me to help,' said the Major, mopping his face. 'Coincidence about Nosey Parker.'

'If you're wasting my time, I'll have you inside, whether or not you know Nosey.'

'Only Bernie can show you properly,' he said. 'I assure you it's all true ... and there he is in jail!'

'You have no other interest? You only wish to assist Mr Weismann?

'Just so!' said the Major.

~

The next day Mary said to Audrey as they sat in the kitchen, 'You could cut the atmosphere with a knife.'

'It wants a good downpour of rain, I suppose,' said Audrey.

'I mean people,' said Mary. 'There's something going on.'

Within a week there was a special sitting of the court and a re-trial, on orders from the government; the outcome of which was that Bernie was released immediately.

When Audrey heard the news she rushed to her father's arms.

'Dad, oh Dad! He's free! When will we be seeing him? Can I see him?'

'Soon, my dear, soon. Yes, you too, of course.'

But she knew instinctively, as Mary had done, that there was something more to the whole thing, although she was not quite sure what.

14

Freedom!

'Bernie, my boy!' said Mr Fellini coming to his table and grasping his hand. 'So now you're a free man; this is a happy day for you! How was the food?'

'The prison food? Not good!'

'How about Today's Special?' He signalled to the waiter. 'Some spaghetti bolognaise for Mr Weismann, and make it one for me. You would not mind if I join you?' he asked, adding: 'This is on the house.'

'That's very kind of you,' said Bernie, smiling.

'And, Alberto,' remonstrated Mr Fellini, 'don't wave those socks about. It don't look good.'

'Without I don't put them in a box, how can I manage?'

'Without you don't put them in nothing!' snapped Mr Fellini. Recovering himself, he said, 'Look, Bernie, why don't you tell me before, you are an Oliphanti?'

'I'm not,' said Bernie.

'You're one of the family. And he's a big man,' added Mr Fellini. 'Everyone know him. I listen to him give a talk, and he call it "The Thing To Do".'

'I heard about it,' said Bernie.

'There's a great difference between an Oliphanti and a Fellini. I come from Napoli. Alberto, he don't know where he come from. And me, I only go back to my grandmother.'

'I understand,' said Bernie.

'Apart from this, we got a great deal in common, and the Major don't know it yet. We both believe in dry feet!'

For a while neither said a word as they dealt with the spaghetti.

'Besides this sock-drying in the kitchen, I've got something big happening with dry feet,' continued Mr Fellini. 'I don't want to talk about it.'

'That suits me, quite honestly,' said Bernie. 'I always heard too much about feet. From Henry, I mean.'

Mr Fellini continued: 'You know when Alberto made me mad just now? When I said, don't wave the socks around, and he said, without he didn't put them in a box how could he help it?'

Bernie nodded.

'Well, he's making a dig at me and nearly letting out a secret that could bring me trouble. That's what I mean. I don't want to talk too much yet.'

'That's fine,' Bernie assured him again.

'It's a Hot Box for Socks. I put wet and sweaty socks in a metal box and get it hot by hanging it in the sun, so they dry out. You're a clever man, Bernie, with all your trials and scoopers I heard about. Check it for me. Tell me what you think.'

'I'll work on it,' said Bernie. 'Nothing occurs to me immediately. Perhaps something like P.H.E.W.! It's the sort of thing people might say when handling the socks.'

'Phew? What is this phew?'

'Patented Hot-boxes for Expelling Water.'

'You're giving them names already? Like this thing Judge Fanshaw get mad about?'

'Like W.H.I.F.F.; that sort of idea,' admitted Bernie.

'I don't mean one of your names; I mean scientific trials,' said Mr Fellini.

'I've a great deal on: I've got to see a government official,' said Bernie. 'Besides, I haven't been out of prison for five minutes yet!'

~

The appointment was at three o'clock.

By eating the spaghetti at Fellini's, Bernie had saved himself the embarrassment of having a long talk with the Major, before meeting the official. Of course there was plenty to discuss, but Bernie could not easily forget the isolation; the lack of friendship over the years, simply because it suited the Major.

He came in quietly by the back door, and said to Mary, 'I'm out.'

She nearly dropped a plate and exclaimed, 'Oh, Mr Weismann, you gave me a fright! Are you all right?' she asked, looking at him closely and taking him by the hand.

'Sure, I'm all right.'

'They thought you might be here for lunch.'

'I went to Fellini's.'

Mary nodded, understanding, then said: 'Seeing the official and getting the government to say it's legal, with you being on the road, it's the sensible way to go about it. I mean, the Major has done the right thing there, at least, hasn't he?'

'I suppose so,' said Bernie, sitting down, 'providing I can carry on with my experiments as I wish.'

'I'll tell them you're here.'

'First, we'll have a cup of tea.'

~

'Thought you might have had lunch with us. The appointment is at three,' the Major said, looking at his watch.

'I'm in good time,' said Bernie. 'I ate at Fellini's.'

'The fellow with the socks. Yes, well, if you're more comfortable there, Bernie ...'

'He admires you; he says dry feet mean much to him also. You've a lot in common!'

Then the door to the sitting room burst open and Audrey rushed in.

'Now this is the moment I've waited for.' Bernie smiled.

The Major said, 'I think we should go over matters before the government man arrives. He's due any minute.'

'Go over what?' asked Bernie.

'And I think we should all just sit down,' said Mrs Oliphant, 'and talk about, well, anything. Not your inventions, Bernie,' she said, touching his hand lightly, 'and not,' she added in a muffled voice, 'wellingtons.'

So Bernie, with Audrey's hand firmly in his, told them of the agreeable characters he had met in prison.

'Can't understand you,' said the Major. 'Try hard. Good people, so forth, how can they be? No respect for the law. Fellows like Fellini, with his wretched socks. There are food hygiene regulations, you know.'

'Henry ...' said Mrs Oliphant.

~

Some time later Audrey was saying: 'Mum, there are people standing at our gates.'

'It's because of the government car.'

'Strange isn't it? I mean, it's only a car, when you think of it.'

'I quite agree,' said Mrs Oliphant, but she was secretly pleased about the fuss. If only Bernie would irritate Henry less!

'Do you know Nosey?' the official had started. He was pacing up and down, now and then looking towards Bernie with suspicion.

'I don't know Nosey. Why should I? Who is he?' asked Bernie.

'I know Nosey,' the Major said anxiously.

'Right!' said the official, sitting down. 'Because the Major here knows Nosey, I've been asked to look into it. What I've heard is that you liquefy methane gas extracted from the ground: from rubbish tips, right?'

'Right,' said Bernie.

'Since it was Mr Weismann, who first thought about using the gas from rubbish tips, I dare say we'll be allowed to travel?' asked the Major anxiously. 'To complete our investigations of course. I've no other interest!'

'We're already using the methane from large infills to generate electricity for the grid. That's been going on for years. It's just that it never has been liquefied on these sites.'

'I use only small sites,' said Bernie.

'Well, do you want my brother-in-law's invention, or not?' asked the Major.

'Henry you don't understand; leave it with me,' said

Bernie. 'The gas is neither here or there, whether it's from a rubbish tip or a digester. It's this liquefying: that means we can use it like petrol!'

The official nodded, saying, 'We liquefy too, Major Oliphant. I thought the position had already been explained to you, when you were rash enough to stop a government car?'

'Fellow said something,' admitted the Major.

'We still have enough North Sea gas to liquefy, but we can't liquefy in small quantities. If our cylinders were stolen, for example, and it's happened before, the fact is that with Mr Weismann's invention here, we could reach an emergency supply ...'

'It's the liquefying of small quantities, Henry,' said Bernie.

'How d'you do it?' asked the official.

'You know, don't you, that the formation of methane in tips and landfills, is due to compression inhibiting ingress of oxygen into its core. OK, so it has to be reached and the first stage of S.M.E.L.L. takes care of this. Then there's the question of the removal of impurities, quite apart from the quite profound cyrogenical problems. Now, what would normally happen is that helium gas enters a reciprocating compressor with an oil free labyrinth piston ...'

'Hold it, Mr Weismann!' the official interrupted. 'I mean in simple terms. I'm not a scientist. I'm here to negotiate an agreement, that's all.'

'I just said it. Simply.'

'You would not interfere with the venting of gas from large sites, used in generating electricity?'

'No, I wouldn't. Besides I like the small sites. One day

all the rubbish tips will be in use.'

'It's certainly less damaging to the atmosphere, using it, rather than letting it escape naturally,' said the official. 'We're interested in that, too.'

'We've brought S.N.I.F.F. up from the cellar to show you,' said the Major.

'Parker told me to look into this particularly. And I don't like it, all this S.M.E.L.L. and S.N.I.F.F. and W.H.I.F.F. business. It's the names. Am I being taken for a ride, gentlemen, just because you know Nosey?'

'I tell you, it's like I said,' Bernie assured him.

'The thing that got me,' said the official, 'was the scooper.'

He cleared his throat, opened his briefcase, and then the discussion started in earnest.

The following was agreed: A government pennant was to be flown from the Bentley's bonnet, at all times, giving freedom of the roads in the UK; all scientific information to do with the extraction of methane and car performance was to be given to officials on request; any engineering work for the further development of devices was to be undertaken in government workshops only. The government did not wish to be involved in any work connected with the scooping of frogs, and Bernie had been able to assure the official that this would not, in any case, be necessary.

Lastly, it was agreed that the manufacture of a number of S.M.E.L.L.s and S.N.I.F.F.s, for government cars, would start immediately in government workshops, which had their own energy supply.

~

After the official had left and the onlookers had drifted away, the Major opened a bottle of old port: one he'd swapped for a pair of size 11's.

'We've deserved it,' he said.

For once, they seemed united.

And for Bernie those first days of freedom went by quickly. Everyone, by now, had heard of him. People, often strangers, came up to him in the street, and customers in Fellini's who had not spoken to him before , shuffled across to his table in their bare feet to shake his hand.

There was much to do, to prepare for his journey: stores to obtain; and so on.

~

Bernie's front room stank of the geraniums, and some ceiling plaster over by the window was bulging.

'It's the weather,' said Bernie.

'When are you going, exactly?' asked Audrey.

'If this rain keeps up, not so soon, maybe,' he shrugged.

That night he walked out on to the Ossington Road. He knew Audrey wanted to travel with him. And Oliver too; he could tell it by looking at him, the way the skin by his eyes pulsed and by his deep silences. So far, they had not asked!

The road stretched ahead under the clear skies. The stars had rarely looked so brilliant.

Audrey, opening her window, had also looked into those skies: How she longed to travel: to the distant plains, to the cool mountains of the north! She thought: if only there was some way of going too!

'I think he wants to do something about wellies as well,' Oliver had pointed out.

And as it continued wet, her dreams faded.

Then the skies cleared. Mist steamed up from the roads and fields.

Mary returned from helping at Bernie's. She said: 'Your uncle sent a message. You and Oliver could walk towards Ossington about three this afternoon, and he'll pick you up for a trial run with that heat imager and scooper thing, if it's all right with your Mum and Dad. Although why Bernie can't come up here and practise, I don't know.'

'He says it's because if he went into town it would cause too much of a stir. You know what it's like, even with goverment cars.'

'Oh well, and maybe he's right,' was all Mary said.

~

'This is as far as we go,' said Bernie, returning after the trial journey, during which both Audrey and Oliver had taken turns reading the information on W.H.I.F.F.

Oliver said excitedly: 'I'm picking up someone now, fifty metres ahead!'

'It looks like my dad,' said Audrey. And indeed it was the Major, out strolling in the sun.

'They could walk back with you,' said Bernie. 'It would be better than going through the town, in this.'

'I say, I feel beastly tired and hot,' the Major protested.

'I do, too,' agreed Bernie, running his finger around his neck. 'I'm sorry.'

'Oh come on, Uncle, please!' said Audrey, 'you've

never tried it.'

'I'd be pleased to take you,' said Bernie. 'But nothing's been seen like this for ages. It's only government cars on certain routes ...'

'Yes, but we're going to other towns soon. We might as well get used to all the fuss,' said the Major.

'I suppose that's true enough,' admitted Bernie.

'Squeeze over, Oliver. It won't be as bad as you think,' said Audrey.

But it was.

~

As soon as they neared Fellini's it became difficult. Bernie had stopped several times, leaning out, smiling, waving his hand, trying to move people on.

The Major who had been staring straight ahead, suddenly jumped out and started shouting, 'Come along, there; move along; now then, a bit sharpish!' And adding, as Bernie, hearing it, hid his face: 'Government car!'

A voice from the crowd, sounding like Bessie Ottershaw's called out: 'It's the old windbag himself!' And the Major spun around angrily, to be greeted unexpectedly by Mr Fellini, who hearing the commotion had come to the door, and cried out: 'Major Oliphanti! How glad I am to meet you: it is you and I keep this town in dry feet!'

The Major looked as if he had been hit over the head.

'I recognise you from the lecture.'

'You what?' said the Major testily.

'Whatta you do!'

'I'm trying to get these people to move,' he replied, not understanding him properly. 'Out of my way, sir!'

Mr Fellini, seeing that he was about to lose the Major, sat down beside him as they began to move off.

Alberto, noticing what was happening, had come out into the street and was angrily waving his arms.

'I cannot work without you come back now!' he shouted. The car was moving forward in a series of short runs. 'Hold on tight, Olly!' Audrey shrieked. In the meantime Mr Fellini continued: 'I don't do my people's socks in these boxes, you understand? The people's socks dry hanging around the cooking stoves. It is a good idea? And this ...' Mr Fellini tapped the box, 'is a better idea even for a gentleman, like yourself. It's a metal box, OK, with a funnel at the top, you see, and a ring to hang it from something.'

The Major was looking flushed.

'The ring,' Mr Fellini repeated, putting his finger in it and swinging the box, 'it is a simple idea, Major Oliphanti. I open the door, so. I put in my socks; hang it outside in the garden and the sun heat the box and the steam from the hot socks comes out of here.' He tapped the funnel.

'Look, my fellow,' began the Major.

'I give it to you,' Mr Fellini's face had become smooth with friendliness. 'I admire you,' he went on.

'It's brilliant, Dad!'

'Bernie!' pleaded the Major.

'He's Mr Fellini,' said Bernie, with a shrug.

'I recognise you,' Mr Fellini beamed, 'And your daughter, Miss Oliphanti.'

'This is Oliver,' said Bernie.

'How do you do, young man,' said Mr Fellini. Turning to the Major, he continued, 'And when I hear you, I ask myself: "What thing?" Then I ask: "What to do?" '

'The Thing To Do,' Bernie explained, as they came to another halt, before moving on.

'What thing?' asked the Major helplessly.

'Is what I say,' joined in Mr Fellini. 'What thing? Is what you also say!'

'He means your lecture,' said Bernie, as they halted again.

'And this,' said Mr Fellini, putting the Hot Box on the Major's lap, 'is what I do! If you have time, Major Oliphanti, perhaps you think about it?'

'I don't want to think about it,' said the Major, who had started to sweat again.

'Bernie, my friend,' said Mr Fellini, 'Alberto is getting excited: I get out now. So nice to meet you, Mr Oliphanti. And Miss Oliphanti; young man!' He leaned close to the Major, saying: 'I begin to make them in my kitchen.'

'Good lord!' whispered the Major.

'Dry feet,' he winked, then squeezed the Major's arm.

~

Bernie had left.

'You'll stay to tea, Oliver?' asked Audrey's mother.

Oliver thanked her and said: 'We met Mr Fellini; what a character!'

'I think he's lovely,' said Audrey. 'It was fun, Dad, wasn't it?'

'Fellini? You see that thing?' He pointed to the Hot Box, which was lying on the floor. 'Criminal activity, that's what. He must know it's against the law to use power to make things.' He thumped the table. 'Bernie mixes with just about anybody. He's so impossible!'

15

George Gives In

George Inkpin lay in his chair in the evening gloom and said: 'I'm tired: it's seeing to all those wellies for recycling.'

'You reckon you've got them all in: here in the town?'

'Oh, yes.' He waved his hand fretfully. 'It's a pity his idea of lecturing didn't work. It would have meant less tramping about. And honestly, I'm worn out.'

'You've worked harder than the Major, I've no doubt,' said his wife.

'Oh, I don't know. We've called at each house, collecting as we went along, and then, when we couldn't carry any more, we'd leave them at the last house, and then start all over again.'

'You doing the carrying?'

'Well, yes. Then the horse and cart would be sent to collect them all up. It worked well.'

'So did you, I've no doubt,' said Mrs Inkpin disapprovingly.

'He's better at talking,' he said. 'But in any case I've

told him I can't go with him and Bernie on those trips they're planning to make.'

Oliver had joined them.

George added: 'I've had enough of it.'

'I'm sure you have,' she said.

'I'm his production manager ... or was. I'm not his welly collector: I'm darned if I am!'

'But Dad, there's no need for you to go, anyway. Couldn't they help each other?' asked Oliver.

'Oh, they could. If they got on. But they don't and they never have,' replied George.

'Yes, that's true,' Oliver agreed.

'The little I know of him,' Mrs Inkpin said, 'I've found Mr Weismann a kind and responsible gentleman. And now, George,' she added, 'if that's what you've done, had words with the Major ...'

'It wasn't like that.'

'Well, told him, then; stick by it! And think of poor Mr Weismann. He'll have to put up with just the Major helping him with those instrument things, I suppose? Isn't that so, Oliver?'

'I'd hoped we could help,' sighed Oliver, 'I know we can do it.'

'Locally, I'm sure that's all right; you and Audrey,' she said. 'But he'll need someone on the long trips. And there's all the wellies to see to as well.'

'Oh, yes,' sighed Oliver, as he thought of S.N.I.F.F., S.M.E.L.L. and W.H.I.F.F. with fondness.

'Perhaps I should ...' said George.

'You're not going anywhere,' said Mrs Inkpin.

'Yes, that's so, I must admit it,' said George, looking at her, his face long and set, glowing from the extra

candles Oliver had lit, talking from his heart. 'Enough
is enough!'

16

Trying Things Out

The man named Rock Petersen was on the tip when Bernie, Oliver, Audrey and the Major arrived for a refuelling exercise which was for the Major's benefit. Petersen's clothes were flapping in the wind that hugged the shapes of smoothed-over rubbish.

'He usually works the fresh rubbish coming in, before it gets covered. Don't you, Rock?' Sticking S.N.I.F.F. into a likely patch and looking at the dial, Bernie went on, 'It's scrap metal he's after, and other bits and pieces. Any luck?' he addressed the ragged man.

'Nothing good, Bernie.' He waved his hands, then fell to looking at the Major, who waited with a dewy moustache and tight pressed mouth behind Bernie, ready to connect S.M.E.L.L.

'You know him?' asked the Major grimly.

'Come on,' said Bernie, 'put the nozzle on!'

'I will, when I'm ready,' said the Major, still being watched by Petersen.

'Who is that disgusting man?' persisted the Major as

he struggled towards S.N.I.F.F.

Bernie said: 'He's got a pile of metal which no-one wants until we get power again. Like you with your old wellies.'

Audrey saw her father fumble with the nozzle. If only, she thought, he would calm down.

The Major's hand was shaking. 'There's no connection.'

'It's there in front of you,' said Bernie. 'Oliver, come over here and show the Major.'

'What is it, Dad?' Audrey said anxiously. 'I had trouble with S.M.E.L.L. at the beginning; don't get all anxious about it.'

'Get away, all of you!' shouted the Major. 'You,' he said to Petersen who had ambled up to the group and was sucking his cheeks in and plainly showing he did not have any teeth. 'Go away, can't you!'

'Dad!' Turning to Mr Petersen she mumbled, 'I'm ever so sorry.'

'And I refuse to call it S.M.E.L.L. Gas liquefier, very well.'

At last it was joined, after a fashion.

'Not used to being stared at by things like that,' the Major added.

'He's a person,' said Bernie. 'He's fine.'

The distances which Audrey turned to look at to hide her shame were dark with rain clouds.

'Before it really comes down, Henry,' said Bernie, looking at the sky, 'd'you want a trip down the Ossington Road, with W.H.I.F.F.?'

'I suppose so,' said the Major, sounding wretched.

'We'll wait in your house, Uncle Bernie. There'll be more room for you, Dad,' said Audrey, knowing that her father was in a state, and would prefer not to be watched.

Cherry was scratching her ear and because of the weather, her dog-oils were smelling more than the geraniums.

'It's no good, you know,' said Audrey. 'I love them both. But it won't be any good.'

~

Mrs Oliphant passed the mint sauce.

'Nice bit of lamb,' said the Major. 'The vicarage ...'

'I beg your pardon?'

'The farm near the vicarage. Rolling hills. Bleating of sheep. Lovely sound. Skipping and frolicking. Sorry they have to go.'

'Who is going, dear?'

'This did: the sheep,' he prodded the meat. 'But it's life.' He prodded it again.

'Is everything all right?' she asked. 'You sound depressed.'

'Nothing's all right. I need people's old wellies. You know that, Priscilla.'

'Yes, I know it,' she said a little sharply.

'Now at last, because of Bernie's car, I will be able to have welly dumps all over the place. And what happens? George walks out on me! And now I'm left with Bernie to help me. And how much time will be left for wellies, I wonder, after I've helped him extract his wretched gas from the tips.'

'But don't you need the gas to get to your wellies, dear?'

'Of course I do,' he snapped.

~

Bernie and the Major were on the way to the town of Ossington, alone, this time to test Bernie's skill at welly collecting.

'Perhaps having everyone looking at you S.N.I.F.F.ing made you nervous,' suggested Bernie.

'Oh, no,' the Major replied. 'In any case, I wasn't sniffing. Stupid way of putting it.'

'There's no need for W.H.I.F.F. until it's dark. But please lower the frog-scooper, okay?'

'Perhaps my trouble is I don't get out enough, Bernie. I should meet more people.'

'We're going to, aren't we, right now? That's why we're going to Ossington. To knock on doors about your wellies.'

'In that sense, yes.'

'I'm not happy,' said Bernie.

'Nor am I all the time,' said the Major.

'I mean with the way you're going to do it.'

'You can't mean that? I bowl 'em over. "I'm Oliphant", I say. If there's a grubby face at the window: "Is that your little boy?" I ask. It's the human touch.'

'I know all that. But the way you do it, you're going to spend all the time organising welly dumps. There won't be much time left for me to travel, and that's what it's all about. That's what I got the pennant for!'

'You wouldn't be doing anything if hadn't been for me getting you out of prison,' the Major smiled irritatingly.

Bernie ignored that. 'And it would be quicker if you did it the right way, like I said,' he persisted. 'There's lots of things you don't do the right way. What about your linings in the foot of the wellies; the sweat absorbers ...'

'What about them?' asked the Major.

'D'you know what they're called in the trade? S.L.A.P.s!'

'I know, of course.'

'I ask you!' said Bernie. 'You don't have a good idea in your head. It stands for Sweat Linings and Absorbers (Patented), right?'

'That is so,' replied the other, shortly.

'Why not Patented Absorbers and Linings for Sweat?... P.A.L.S.! Who wants a S.L.A.P.? Put P.A.L.S. in your wellyphants: that's the way to go about it.'

The Major said nothing, reminding himself that he had to get on with Bernie. Yesterday he had been ready to give up. That man Petersen ... Bernie's friends!

I have to get on with Bernie, he thought again, reminding himself of the fortune that awaited him.

~

In Ossington it had started miserably for Bernie, who had insisted on working alone, when first trying out the Major's methods, as much as he disagreed with them.

'How is your little boy?' he asked a lady who had been in the middle of making a meat stew.

'He's all right,' she said, wiping her hands, as a sudden waft of onion escaped through the opened door; anxious to get back to the kitchen while the power was still on.

'Yes, he's fine,' she added, waiting.

'What's his name?' asked Bernie.

'I'll just get my husband.'

Bernie could hear the sound of muffled voices from

the kitchen, then a voice saying: 'I'll tell him.'

'I'm Bert,' said a large man.

'Bernie.'

'We've just been doing the onions. Excuse the smell,' he said with an evil looking smile and then taking Bernie's hand, crushed it. 'He's Stephen.'

'Have you got any wellies in your shed?' Bernie asked, biting his lips in pain.

~

'How was it?' asked the Major.

'Not so good.'

'Try again. As before; won't watch you. Know how it feels.'

And this time it had been different. He had been just Bernie Weismann. And they listened! He had collected names and addresses to give to the man with the horse and cart, having left up to 6 pairs at each house.

'Good,' said the Major, looking at the list.

'But I didn't do it your way: you're not doing it right, like I said,' said Bernie.

'I'm what?'

'First,' he said, 'people don't want this "How's your little boy?" business, this "What are you cooking?" All the questions.'

'Puts people at their ease.'

'Not when I do it,' said Bernie. 'And another thing, the certificates with the five per cent off. You'll only put it on in the first place and then take it off later. Or you could make your wellies longer and mark it, "This bit free". It's all tricks. People are not stupid.'

'I know what I'm doing,' said the Major, controlling

his temper.

'Likewise I do,' said Bernie, 'I just say to people, look, I'm Bernie Weismann. What's that to you? Nothing! I want to recycle wellies. There's all this junk lying every-where spoiling the face of the earth. "Sure," they say. People like recycling. They love the earth, most people, even if it's a little late. But in any case,' said Bernie, 'it will take too long ... the way you do it, or even the way I do it. It's no good for me.'

'I don't want to make your position difficult, Bernie, but ... '

'You need George to help you with wellies, while I get on with my work.'

'He won't, you know that.' Scarcely able to contain his anger the Major added, 'Your attitude is unhelpful.'

As they came to the straight road Bernie increased speed. By now the stars were shining palely; trees and hedgerows stood out black.

It was the sort of night Bernie loved. It was often like this, in between the rain.

'Switch on W.H.I.F.F.' he called out, as the engine roared.

But a second later, he had brought the Bentley to a screeching stop.

'I told you to put the scooper down. Ages ago I told you!'

'What's the matter?' the Major asked dully.

'Frogs! We've killed hundreds probably, thanks to you!'

'Do you think I care about a lot of dead frogs?' shouted the Major. 'Do you think I care about your W.H.I.F.F.? Take me home!'

17

'I Simply Can't Go'

Weeks had gone by and now everyone was waiting for the government car; for Nosey's men, who had been due to come to the town that day to deliver the latest of Bernie's inventions.

'It's very distressing not knowing when Mr Parker's people are coming,' said Mrs Oliphant.

'I only gave them the drawing of it a couple of weeks ago,' said Bernie. 'Maybe they need more time.'

'I expect it will be next week, Henry,' Mrs Oliphant said, trying to reassure her husband.

'Bernie, you know, if it hadn't been for this wretched new device of yours, we'd have been on the road by now,' protested the Major.

'You want me to help with the wellies, right?' said Bernie. 'So the whole thing has to be speeded up ... there isn't time for you to go S.N.I.F.F.ing around, especially the way you do it.'

'What do you mean?' asked the Major, flushing.

'It is a little bit difficult, Uncle, you know, especially

the first time,' said Audrey.

'This ... thing,' said the Major, 'it just speeds it up?'

'You don't mean you're doing away with S.N.I.F.F.?' Audrey asked.

'No, no!' said Bernie. 'It makes S.N.I.F.F.'s job easier, that's all.'

'Is it really necessary, though? Dad's getting awfully anxious.'

'Can you blame me?' asked the Major. 'We've just got to get at those wellies. No time to lose!'

'What does it do?' Audrey asked.

'I tell you later, some day, when it's delivered,' said Bernie.

'What do you call it, then?' she persisted.

'I hoped you would not ask me. I call it S.T.I.N.K.'

'When Parker's men have left your S.T.I.N.K.,' said the Major, struggling with his temper, 'we'll be ready to go?'

'No reason why not,' said Bernie.

Audrey thought: well, I can think of one ... the way you go on at each other! You'll never stand it!

~

'Another thing,' said the Major after Bernie had left and Audrey had gone into the kitchen, 'if Nosey himself turns up next week, how do I explain Bernie? What sort of a man calls a thing a S.T.I.N.K.?'

'It stands for something,' said Priscilla.

'Of course it does. But he makes the description fit peculiar words. It's not true about the lozenges, for a start.'

'We all have our little peculiarities. Nosey will know

and understand, dear.'

After a while he added: 'Maybe a week's delay is just as well, after all.'

He needed time to master Bernie's equipment! For a moment he wondered about himself: was anything wrong? Audrey and Oliver could manage all of it; W.H.I.F.F. and everything. Surely adults took longer? Known fact. Surely, he wondered, with a feeling of panic, this was so?

Or could people like Alberto or even Petersen do it?

~

Later the same day, Bernie was stretching his feet under one of Mr Fellini's tables. He had taken his shoes off.

'You don't mind if I join you?' Mr Fellini asked, pulling out a chair.

'Sure,' said Bernie, waving his hand.

'Alberto, take Mr Weismann's socks.'

'My socks are OK,' said Bernie.

'Please,' said Alberto, trembling, 'do I take these socks or not?'

'Leave it,' said Mr Fellini, adding when his waiter was out of earshot. 'He gets too worked up. Look at him!'

'He needs a break, maybe? Maybe one afternoon I could take him down the Ossington Road?'

'He says he don't like serving food and doing socks at the same time.'

'When the power comes back, government food inspectors won't like him doing it either.'

'Alberto is talking just about overwork.'

'There will be power soon, though,' said Bernie.

'Then people won't want no socks dried over my kitchen range: they dry them at home. Maybe they also use my Hot Boxes,' said Mr Fellini.

'When there's power again, people won't want your Hot Boxes,' Bernie warned.

'In the meantime,' said Mr Fellini, 'I strike the iron while it's hot.'

'You and Henry should get together,' he smiled.

~

As he left, he turned to Mr Fellini, looking deeply saddened. 'Enjoy these times; I tell you, we'll look back at the candle-light and Alberto trying to find the owners of socks ...'

'Maybe you're right, Bernie.'

'And everybody who comes in here for company, and the parties in the street, and the good wholesome food, and no cars on the road ...'

'I want to get together with you on frogs. The legs taste good.'

'It's not like that,' said Bernie.

As they came out into the street together, Bernie suddenly put his arms around Mr Fellini's shoulder, saying, 'I tell you, enjoy these times, before life gets back to where it was!'

As they embraced, Major Oliphant happened to be stepping out briskly on the other side of the road, still furious at his brother-in-law's behaviour. He carried on, hoping that he had not been seen, and went into the first café he saw, to recover from the shock. Bernie was the last person he wished to see.

'Tea,' he said starting to sweat again.

'Scones? Bacon butties?'

'No, no: tea.'

'Nettle? Herb teas, it's all we do.'

'Oh yes, nettle tea then.'

He was impossible! And now he was apparently on friendly terms with Fellini; actually hugging the man! Friends with Petersen. Talking to Mary like that, in his own sitting room. Audrey having tea with the Inkpins; it was as if St Cuthbert's had never existed, the way things were.

He said to the waitress: 'This cup is cracked.'

'Take it or leave it,' she replied.

Miserably, he thought: if it's like this now, with Bernie; how are we going to manage on our travels?

~

Worse was to follow. One evening, a few days later, Mary asked: 'Anything else?'

'No, thank you,' said Mrs Oliphant.

'In that case, seeing as that's all, you've a visitor. I put him in the hall.'

'Who is it?' asked the Major.

'Mr Fellini.'

'Show him out again!' he said.

'You can't do that, Henry.'

'I'm asking Mary to.'

'I'm not,' said Mary.

'Oh my goodness me,' he said as he came to terms with it.

~

'Major Oliphanti! Mrs Oliphanti!' He ceased bowing, then beamed at Audrey, adding: 'Miss Oliphanti!'

'Hello, Mr Fellini. What fun!' she added, unable to contain herself.

'Is what fun?'

'I mean it's nice.'

'Is very nice. It is my pleasure! Major Oliphanti!'

'Phant,' said the Major showing signs of irritation.

'What is phant?'

'Mr Fellini, do please take a seat,' said Mrs Oliphant. 'Would you like a cup of nettle tea? Milk and sugar?'

'Thank you, thank you,' he said. 'Major Oliphanti, I come to ask you how you get on with my Hot Box. And something else also. You already are asking yourself, what thing? I bet.'

'No, Mr Fellini, you are mistaken,' he said with the cold courtesy reserved for servants and such people.

'You like ...' he paused, turning to Mrs Oliphant, 'you forgive me please. Major Oliphanti, you like hot socks?'

As the colour drained from the Major's face and neck, he merely blinked.

'Nice dry socks?' he repeated. 'I have sold fourteen Hot Boxes. But of course my spaghetti comes first.'

'You make spaghetti, Mr Fellini? How interesting!' said Mrs Oliphant.

'Spaghetti with meat balls, spaghetti al burro, spaghetti milanese, spaghetti napolitana. You name it; we've got it. Also I do egg and chips, pork sausages with chips ...'

'Lovely!' said Audrey.

'When I say to Bernie, "I strike the iron while it is hot," he said to me you and Henry should get together. Mr

Weismann ... he thinks we have something in common.' Here Mr Fellini bowed slightly, feeling that he might have overstepped the mark, then went on: 'What thing? you ask ... Is dry feet, Major Oliphanti! Bricks and chimney pots over your head; food, whatever you like, spaghetti, chips, anything; people you love: Mrs Oliphanti, Miss Oliphanti; but if you don't have dry feet, you don't have nothing!'

'Splendid to hear your views, Mr Fellini,' said the Major, rising to his feet.

'All the other things, they go phut!'

'Dad, you've often said the same thing. Well, sort of, anyway. In a different way, at least.'

'Endlessly,' added Mrs Oliphant.

'I knew it!' said Mr Fellini.

'Is that all?'

'Perhaps you like to drop in one day?'

'That would be fine,' said Audrey, biting her lip. 'Wouldn't it, Dad?'

'There's one other thing,' said Mr Fellini.

'What thing?' asked the Major, unwisely.

Mr Fellini chuckled with approval. 'It's good! What thing? you ask. Mrs Oliphanti, you hear about this The Thing To Do?'

'What thing?' said Mrs Oliphant.

'Please, Mr Fellini, what is it that you wish to tell me? Your presence here this afternoon, although unexpected, has braced me up considerably. But I must now be getting along.' As he spoke, the Major's mouth twitched convulsively.

'I wish,' said Mr Fellini, 'because we have our hearts so much together in dry feet, to do you a little kindness.

I wish to give you Alberto.'

'Who is Alberto?' asked the Major in a barely audible voice.

'Is my waiter.'

'Why?' asked the Major, gripping the sideboard.

'Bernie said you don't get on with W.H.I.F.F.'

'He said that?'

'I give you Alberto: on your welly trip. I got a man called Petersen to look after the socks, and I do the waiting and forget my Hot Boxes. They're only a side line anyway.'

'I'm sure they polish up nicely. We've still got ours, haven't we, Henry?'

'What?'

'Mr Fellini's Hot Box.'

'Why do you want to give me Alberto?' asked the Major, who was now beginning to look quite ill.

'Bernie took him out for a trip. He didn't tell you that? He's been working too hard. He don't like doing the two things together. Socks or spaghetti, he says. And he gets on real good with W.H.I.F.F. Alberto is shouting his head off down the Ossington Road.'

'I can't stand it,' said the Major.

Audrey, knowing all the signs, took Mr Fellini's arm, saying, 'This way, Mr Fellini!'

And with Mrs Oliphant saying loudly, 'So nice of you to call. So nice. So very, very nice,' they both managed to drown the Major's last words.

'Get out of here!' he said.

~

All through the following week they left him alone. Mary had taken to popping her head in during meals and then with a glance at the Major, and thinking silence was best, would form the words 'Anything else?' at Mrs Oliphant, silently with her mouth and with a great deal of exaggeration.

He caught her at it.

'What's the matter with you?'

'Nothing.'

'Come, come, Mary. With your mouth; the thing you were doing.'

'What thing?'

'What do you mean, "What thing"?' he asked, going white.

'Henry, you cannot expect people to get rid of entire strings of words from the English language because for some reason they are painful to you.'

'Mr Fellini said it was a very good lecture, Dad,' Audrey interrupted, reassuring him.

'Maybe so, maybe so,' said the Major.

'Your father needs bolstering up,' said Mrs Oliphant later.

~

The door to St Michael's was open, so the Major went in. The smell of damp prayer books tickled his nose. He stood for a moment, making sure that he was alone, then walked thoughtfully towards the marble busts of his ancestors. He stopped at each one, hands behind his back, fingers clasped, breathing deeply, mouth pressed tight and lips pushing out as if in silent conversation with them.

Whatever he did, he could not concentrate. He ached.

He made his way towards Sir Thomas and his wife and stood in the rays of the sun. He felt Lady Judith's broken nose. His fingers clutched at it. He was weeping.

The nose was warm from the sunlight. The tears were rolling down his cheeks, and the pain in his chest had gone.

All right, he thought. So, Alberto could use W.H.I.F.F. Well, he was an Oliphant ... good at wellies. Couldn't be good at everything; not natural. No good at getting on with Bernie. He couldn't stand the man!

No, he could not do it!

Nor could he hob-nob with Fellini and all Bernie's friends and people like them. Very well, it meant a fortune lost. But no, he could not!

There would be no wellyphants! No recycling. No fortune. Bernie must go on his own, with his wretched inventions.

'I can't,' he cried out, knowing that he was defeated. 'I simply can't do it!'

~

At that moment, to the Major's astonishment, the vicar stepped out of the shadows by the vestry and coming towards him, with his arms widespread, said:

'What is it, Simon?'

'Just a bit of play-acting,' said the Major. 'How did you like it?'

'Like what?' asked the vicar.

The Major said, 'By the way, I'm not Simon.'

'No, of course.'

'I'm Henry.'

'I realise that.'

'Practising a bit of dramatics. Amateur dramatics, you know.'

'I didn't know you were a member,' said the vicar truthfully.

'I'm not yet. This is my piece. "I can't," he said, but this time conversationally, "I simply can't do it!" Should be signed up, don't you think?'

'I'll put in a word for you,' said the vicar. 'I know the producer.'

'Of course, shouldn't have used the church. But Priscilla is a bit touchy these days.'

'Oh dear, I'm sorry to hear that. Audrey well?'

'Oh yes; well.'

'Ah!' He paused. 'For a moment, Major, I had thought ...' And then he had spoken about the church fête and the matter passed.

The Major returned home exhausted, but free at last of uncertainty; almost grateful now to Mr Fellini for having brought matters to a head; grateful too for the delay caused by Bernie's new invention ... Without it, he might have been on the road by now, and stuck with his brother-in-law's company!

It all came back, one way or the other, to Bernie and his ideas on equality. Even the vicar had suddenly decided to call him by his forename, or at least what he had supposed it was.

'D'you know what, Priscilla?'

'What, dear?'

'The vicar called me Simon. You'd think the poor fellow would know I'm Henry. I said, "I'm Henry," and he said "Of course". What d'you make of that?'

Audrey said, after a moment's thought, 'What did he say exactly, Dad?'

'What is it, Simon?'

'Where were you, Dad?' asked Audrey.

'Standing by Sir Edwin, if you must know.'

'The vicar's getting old, dear.'

'I don't like all this familiarity, Priscilla.'

'We live in changed times, Henry,' she said.

Audrey looked at her father carefully, but said nothing.

~

The sound of frogs was in the wind. It was a curious rhythm, with pauses enough for Audrey to hear the rain washing down. Then they would start again.

Shutting her window, she went to her father's study.

'Dad, I'm going to the Inkpins for tea.'

'I've not seen George for some time. He's all right?'

'Yes.'

'You'll need your umbrella.'

'I know.'

'Something interesting, I hope.' He knew he had been short with Audrey of late; that it had been unreasonable to ask her to see less of Oliver. 'Boiled eggs, I expect?'

'I would think so, yes. Cakes too, I've no doubt: she's invited some neighbours.' Audrey paused. 'Dad ...'

The Major looked at her, waiting. He got up and closed the window. 'Damn frogs,' he said.

'When are you going?' she asked.

'Where?'

'With Uncle Bernie.'

'Not until his new invention arrives,' he said, beginning to shift uneasily.

'Oh, Dad, couldn't we go, Oliver and I? You can concentrate on wellies, which is a far more important and we can help Uncle Bernie; Oliver's awfully good with W.H.I.F.F. and the rest.'

'No you cannot! You cannot, d'you hear?' he said in a strained voice. 'I'm perfectly capable of doing it myself; perfectly, d'you understand?'

Audrey went to him and put her arm round his neck, saying, 'Oh Dad, what is it?'

He did not answer. He muttered, as if Audrey was not there, 'I simply can't do it!'

And again she said, 'What is it?' No reply. She bent down and kissed him lightly, then left the room.

18

Audrey to the Rescue

By the time Audrey had reached the Inkpins, the sun was out from behind the clouds and the vapour was rising from the sodden sheds and the dazzling slate roofs. On walls and by the rickety front gates cats were curled up, as if waiting for the next day.

'Audrey, you sit here, dear, will you?' said Mrs Inkpin. 'Oliver, you go next to your Dad. Dotty: that all right?' she said indicating a brown leather chair to Mrs Crabbe. Mrs Crabbe was one of the Inkpins' neighbours.

'Dolly Perkins is coming soon,' said Mrs Crabbe. 'I've just been in there and she's 'aving a bit of an argy-bargy with her old man.'

'Oh, well,' said Mrs Inkpin. 'Mavis, you could go next to Audrey.'

Sitting down, Mavis explained: 'I'm Mrs Crabbe's niece.'

'An Avon Lady, Audrey dear,' said Mrs Crabbe, allowing her dentures to drop by mistake.

'I was.' Mavis smiled. 'But not any more.'

'Not just an ordinary Avon Lady, dear,' said Mrs Crabbe, cracking her egg with a spoon. Her cheeks and forehead were glistening. 'But in charge of all the Avon Ladies, all over.'

'What d'you mean, "all over", Dotty?' asked Mrs Inkpin.

'The county.'

'I was the county organiser, that's all,' said Mavis. 'Auntie, it's not all that interesting.'

'Faces is, dear,' said Mrs Crabbe, 'and the beautifying of them.'

'Wasn't it about ladies coming to your home and selling beauty preparations and so on?' Audrey asked.

'I 'ave just the thing for you, Madam,' mimicked Mrs Crabbe.

'That's right,' Mavis said.

'And you were in charge of them all? Are there Avon Ladies everywhere?' asked Audrey with interest.

'There were. But not any more: not working, at least,' said Mavis.

'There will be again, you mark my words. All that vanishing cream. Get rid of all them bits of scraggy skin.'

'Oh, Auntie!' said Mavis.

'Things'll get back to where they were,' said her aunt.

'No,' Mr Inkpin interrupted, 'it will never be quite the same again, even when we have the new power. In any case, it had better not be ... look at the mess we've got ourselves into!'

'He gets gloomy, sometimes,' said Mrs Inkpin. 'Don't you, Dad?' adding, 'Come on, help yourselves. Don't stand on ceremony!'

Just then, there was a commotion by the back door. Mrs Perkins, red-faced, came in supporting Mr Perkins.

Oliver and his parents jumped up to assist. 'Are you all right, Dolly?' enquired Mrs Crabbe.

'Course I am, but is he, the cantankerous old man! Mr Inkpin, I'm ever so sorry!'

Audrey said: 'Gosh, Mr Perkins, you'd better have my seat.'

'Whatever made you do it?' Mrs Inkpin asked the old man when his breathing had settled down. 'I've never seen you out of bed in all these years,' adding, 'd'you let him have cream cakes, Dolly?'

'It's on account of this young lady,' said Mrs Perkins, nodding at Audrey, 'and him just finding out she's an Oliphant, and him being a welly trimmer all those years back in the days of Major Oliphant's father, and remembering all the other welly trimmers. They were his mates, you see.'

'Will you have some cream cake, Mr Perkins?' asked Mrs Inkpin.

'Just one will do him nicely,' said Dolly Perkins.

'It's indigestion,' said Mr Perkins, leaning towards Audrey.

Then he spoke to Audrey, just the two of them together, of welly trimming long ago, when wellies were made of rubber. Finally Mrs Perkins was saying, 'Come along, she doesn't want to hear all that.'

Everyone started to leave at once.

'It's been nice, Olly,' sighed Audrey. 'Dad's in a state.'

'What's up, this time?'

'Not being able to use W.H.I.F.F. I think. I'm not sure. I'm very worried about him sometimes. I'd do anything to help, especially with wellies ... they mean so much to him.'

'If you're passing my house, look me up,' Mavis was saying.

'You live in town?' asked Audrey.

'I do,' said Mavis. She fished in her handbag. 'One of my old cards. This is me; look.' It read: Avon Ladies County Controller ... Mavis Longbotham.

Before leaving, Audrey, accompanied by Oliver, helped Mrs Perkins return Mr Perkins to his bed. After Mrs Perkins had gone downstairs, the old man requested Oliver to bring over a jar containing peppermints.

'They're good for indigestion. Mrs Perkins makes them herself. Would you have one Oliver, and you Audrey? I may call you Audrey; you too will have one? I am lucky to have Mrs Perkins.'

Then, Audrey bent forward and for the second time that day kissed with a gentle kiss and a heart that was even fuller than before.

~

On her return she found the Major sitting in his study, in darkness: he had not even bothered to light a candle. After lighting one, she closed the windows to deaden the sound of frogs, which seemed to be irritating her father more and more these days.

If only, asking him: 'what is it, Dad?' she could get a truthful answer! And, she wondered, had he unburdened himself when the vicar had asked, or rather had meant to ask, as she alone had guessed, not 'What is it, "Si-mon"?' but 'What is it, my son?' She doubted it!

'The government car has been. They delivered it. Your uncle's invention is here,' he said at last.

'Oh, I see,' she said. 'But surely that's marvellous, isn't it?'

'Audrey, there's something you and you mother must know. I can't do it.'

'What can't you do, Dad?'

Mrs Oliphant had joined them.

'I'm not going to do it. The fact is, I simply can't,' repeated the Major.

'What can't you do, dear?'

'Go. I am not going with Bernie. I have no desire to go. l do not wish to lead the sort of life he leads. I do not share his views. No welly piles. No fortune. All lost.'

'But S.T.I.N.K.'s here, Dad,' said Audrey.

'What's wrong with Bernie, now?' asked Mrs Oliphant.

'What sort of man would take his socks off, like that?' cried the Major.

'He's my brother,' Mrs Oliphant replied, adding with impatience, 'and why not ask him to see to the welly piles, if you can't stand his company? Well, why not?'

'Interested only in his inventions. Would do nothing about wellies without me. You know that.'

Mrs Oliphant said: 'It's true, of course.'

'Mum, Dad, if we went; if Oliver and I went with Uncle Bernie, I mean it would only be for a week at a time; he said so.' She paused, almost against her will, waiting for his anger, as if inviting it, but there was none; no response. He sat motionless.

She went on, now confidently, almost measuring the time it was taking for her words to spill out, 'You see, as you would say, I'm an Oliphant, and, yes, I would look after the wellies: you're right, Mum. I think Uncle Bernie wouldn't, quite so much. I would make sure that wherever we went, everyone in the town or city or whatever would soon know about the wellies. And I'm sure Uncle Bernie would plan where the welly piles should be. And Oliver's ever so good with W.H.I.F.F. and S.M.E.L.L. and S.N.I.F.F. and I'm sure we will be with S.T.I.N.K. as well, whatever that is; and really, I am, too; because, Dad, young people are better at this sort of thing. That's all it is.'

'Wellyphants,' the Major murmured, 'what a name!'

'Exactly!' she said. 'And I have an idea. It occured to me when Mrs Crabbe's niece was telling me about the Avon Ladies. They sound wonderful people: they go everywhere. I'm sure Mavis would help make it work. And with S.T.I.N.K. speeding things up and the Avon Ladies calling everywhere about old wellies ... Think of it, Dad!'

Audrey broke the silence which followed. 'You don't mind, Mum? Let Oliver and me go, Dad, and help Uncle Bernie!'

'If the Inkpins ...'

'They're happy about it. I know that already.'

'I have no more objections to it,' he said wearily. 'None.'

19

A Great Party

Bernie was at Fellini's.

'Here, Alberto, my socks,' he said.

'You ready to go on your travels, Bernie?' Mr Fellini asked.

'Two days. Three, maybe.'

'We'll have a celebration before you leave!'

In the woods and everywhere it seemed as quiet as death. Behind Bernie's, the yellowing chestnut leaves fell crookedly in the still air. Now that the car was loaded and the supplies were strapped in, Bernie had more time to think about Audrey's plan concerning Mavis.

Audrey had met Mavis again, and both she and Oliver were impressed. Miss Longbotham had given them the names and addresses not only of the Ladies in her own county, but also of other county organisers, all of whom would be able to put them in touch with *their* Avon Ladies.

'So these Ladies do all the calling on houses,' Bernie

said. 'And they do it for nothing?'

'We'll take some new wellies with us,' said Audrey. 'Dad thought one pair for every 1000 pairs collected.'

'That's not over-generous.'

'He's right; and we can't carry that many. And Mavis says she's sure her own Ladies will all want to support recycling and will welcome the chance to meet people at the doorstep again.'

'Sure, OK,' said Bernie. 'So we'll need something like a horse-box which we can lock. And we could put S.T.I.N.K. into it, as well.'

'What exactly is it?' Oliver asked with a sigh.

'It scans the inside of rubbish tips.'

'Closed circuit television?' Oliver queried.

'But what for, Uncle?' asked Audrey. 'It's just the gas you want; why worry about what the inside looks like?'

'Tell me more about Mavis.'

'Uncle!'

'OK! You'd see old cookers standing up in spaces where everything else has rotted; ceilings made up of old mattresses; that sort of thing. And we'd know where it's better to put S.N.I.F.F. Now please tell me,' said Bernie, changing the subject, 'how many pairs of wellies are we taking?'

'That's up to Dad.'

'And these Ladies are everywhere?'

'In every city and in most towns in the UK,' replied Audrey. 'And what is so special about S.T.I.N.K. that you're not telling us what it means?

'The name's not so good,' said Bernie. 'It took me a long time to think of it. I thought of W.H.I.F.F. and all the others at odd moments, like when I was taking off my socks. It was easy.'

'Why keep it to that sort of thing, if it is so difficult?' asked Audrey.

'It's a series. Like you get Beechwood Avenue, Oak Tree Close, Birch Road; you know? I can't use just any old name. You wouldn't know the Dutch word *kopje*? It means a small hill.'

'I've never heard of it,' admitted Audrey.

'I'm running out of ideas for names of this kind,' said Bernie as his eyebrows wobbled with agitation.

'Why bother at all?' she persisted.

'The Ossington tip has plenty of these small hills,' he went on. 'The full name is Sensored: meaning, of course, that it has instruments which respond to and signal a change in physical condition ...'

'I'm sure it's quite brilliant, Uncle. But all the same!'

'I do it for relaxation. It's a strain. Look, without it, I take life too seriously!'

'We understand,' said Oliver. 'So, what is it, Bernie?'

'Sensored and Televised Interiors of Nauseating Kopjes.'

'Well ... yes,' said Audrey.

'It's a harmless pursuit,' said Bernie, clasping his hands together. 'I need to do it.'

For a while they sat in silence. Then he said: 'I'm glad you've sorted out something with this Mavis. It sounds like a good idea. And Henry will get his welly piles: I'll see to that, my dear.'

~

'An invitation from Fellini,' said the Major contemptuously, letting a card drop from his hand.

'It's in honour of Uncle Bernie,' Audrey explained.

'I'm not going to it, you may be sure!'

'It's to celebrate the expedition generally, Dad, and S.T.I.N.K.'s arrival and all that. It's for me and Oliver, as well.'

'At Fellini's, Audrey? Really!'

'I think you should consider it, Henry. It would be a fine gesture on your part.'

'Mary's going,' said Audrey.

The Major looked at her; shook his head and sighed.

'And Oliver's parents. Well, then, can you come, Mum?'

'We'll see,' said Mrs Oliphant uncertainly.

~

It was late on the morning of the party. Cherry lay quivering in her basket, knowing that Bernie's car was packed and that even her dog bowl was on board. Petersen was making his way slowly in to town from the Ossington tip, having left his hut made of tin and old carpets. A smell of cooking hung in a pall over Fellini's. Mrs Oliphant was resting in her sitting room. She was scratching her neck and was in a pitiable condition, as she said to Audrey, 'My dear, I cannot go!'

'Poor Mum; of course you can't. Don't worry; I'll say goodbye now. See you in a week. And thanks for letting me go; both of you. I'll make sure everything goes all right with the wellies; I know it means everything to Dad.'

'Your father is happy with the idea, and the way it's

turned out with the Avon Ladies. It's a great relief to him. What a wonderful organisation that must be.'

'Meanwhile, what about you, Mum?' Audrey said.

'I'm seeing the doctor again, although all they can suggest these days are herbal remedies. If any of the Avon Ladies happen to have an old pot of cream to spare, don't forget me, will you? And now goodbye, my love!'

They embraced, then Audrey said: 'Now I must see Dad.'

'He's gone.'

'He's what?'

'Oh, yes! He should have told you; he's left for Fellini's. I think he imagined you'd be down there already.'

'So he's gone to Fellini's! I didn't think for one minute ... well, that's unbelievable!'

'See that he relaxes, dear. As you can guess, he's doing it just for you. He's fretted about it these last few days.' She started to scratch her neck. 'You're still his only child. Look after yourself!'

~

'Miss Oliphanti!' exclaimed Mr Fellini, striding towards her.

'I wish you'd call me Audrey.'

'And I'm Eduardo, Eduardo Fellini,' he said, the gold filling in his back teeth showing; 'and why not?'

'Why not, indeed?' said Audrey.

'You go to the top table.'

'I'm a little late.'

Then, to her great distress he called out: 'Miss Audrey Oliphanti!'

A place had been kept for her. Oliver was on one side of Bernie and she on the other and next to Mrs Inkpin. The Major was seated by Oliver, but try as she might she could not get her father's attention.

'Mr Fellini has done it very well, I must say,' said Mrs Inkpin. 'Very thoughtful of him to have got all the family at one table.'

'I'm not family, dear,' said Mrs Crabbe, leaning across to Audrey.

'We know you're not, Dotty,' said Mrs Inkpin.

'I said if I wasn't going to sit here, I'd go 'ome again. If Dolly Perkins had been able to come, she'd 'ave said the same.'

'I'm sure it's all for the best,' said Mrs Inkpin. 'Well, Audrey, are you looking forward to it?'

'You bet I am!'

'So you should be,' said Mrs Crabbe. 'The furthest I've been since all this happened to the electric, is Ossington.'

Then the Major glanced at Audrey and she smiled and said 'Good to see you!' although she was not sure if he had heard.

He was staring past her, looking tired. Occasionally he pulled out a handkerchief and mopped his face. Mr Fellini came up to him and Audrey could just hear him reply, 'Yes fine. Everything's fine.'

~

The Major's attention had been drawn by the appearance of a new arrival: a dishevelled figure seated at the next table. It was Petersen. The old man saw the Major looking at him and, not deterred, drew forth from the folds of his jacket a silver-plated flask. He unscrewed this, then closing his eyes, smelled it. He drank from it, carefully replaced the top, returning the Major's look at the same time; then wiped his mouth on his sleeve.

Alberto had now gone to Petersen.

'The soup's finished,' he said. 'You want spaghetti with meat balls? Spaghetti al burro, spaghetti milanese, spaghetti napolitana? As the boss says, "You name it, we got it!" '

Petersen struggled to reply. Finally he said: 'Beans on toast.'

'We don't have it.'

'Give him meat balls,' someone suggested helpfully.

'OK. One meat balls. Anything to go with it?' Petersen said: 'Give this to him over there.' He handed Alberto the flask, adding, 'D'you want my socks?'

'I don't take no socks now,' Alberto snapped.

'Bring it back when he's had some,' said Petersen.

'It's for you, Major,' said Alberto, beginning to fume. 'I'm to wait and take it back. How can I see to my work and do this also?'

'What is it?'

'It's from Mr Weismann's friend, over there. Him from the tip,' said Alberto disdainfully. 'It's probably home-made wine.'

'Take it away,' said the Major, looking unwell.

'Why is he here?' he asked Bernie.

'Because he's kept me company on many long afternoons on the tip,' said Bernie.

Audrey then got up and came over to him. She took his hand, saying,'Dad, I'm so glad you came.'

After the pudding, one or two had got up to walk

around.

'I tell you what,' said Mary, handing Bernie a bottle of wine, 'have this on your table and make sure the Major has some; it's what my cousin has just given me. Yes, he's here, I'm afraid,' she added. 'And he owes the Major a drink considering all the ham he's had off him.'

Someone started to play a guitar, then there were cries of 'sssh' everybody!' as Mr Fellini stood on a chair. Alberto was leaning against the door leading into the kitchen, with a tea towel on his shoulder, and drenched with sweat.

'Please, everybody! My good friend Bernie Weismann with Oliver Inkpin and Audrey Oliphanti are going on a journey of great importance.'

'We know; get on with it!' someone called.

'All right, so we can't all be as clever as Bernie, but we must try to do something for the state of the world. I, Fellini, do my hot socks. I say to myself: What thing; What must I do? But what you may ask is my dry socks service compared with Major Oliphanti's wellingtons? He say, What thing? Recycle old wellies, is the thing to do!

'So, first of all, Bernie, with his helpers, goes to test his inventions, then also to make welly piles. Ladies and gentlemen ... a toast to Mr Bernie Weismann! To Audrey Oliphanti and Oliver Inkpin!'

Then Bernie spoke and was received with much affection, particularly by Mary, who had always thought him hard done by, by his family.

Meanwhile, the Major had descended further into gloom. He responded each time he met Audrey's gaze with a fixed smile.

He hardly heard the words: 'And now my brother-in-law, Major Oliphant.'

~

Whether it was the Major's brooding appearance or his manner, is not certain. But whereas the other speakers had been encouraged, he had been met with silence. He spoke of the joys of wearing wellington boots. He made the remark that if you had everything in this world that you wanted and you had not got dry feet, then what was the point of it all?

To make matters worse, there in front of him was Bessie Ottershaw. She had opened her handbag and now stood up in the room, waving her welly trimming knife over her head, shouting: 'And who's made a fortune out of it? Who's been taking sides of pigs, all sorts, in exchange for new wellies? Who's made a fortune already and now wants to make another, with his recycling?'

There was a stunned silence after this outburst. Audrey saw at once how tired and upset her father looked. Then a voice chanted, 'But if you don't have dry feet, what's the point of it all?'

Then Mr Fellini stood up and said, as Audrey winced, 'You have a charming wife, and a pretty daughter; you have pigs hanging up, you have everything you want, and you don't have dry feet, then you don't have nothing!'

Audrey pulled her chair closer to her father's side. Suddenly he had found the heat unbearable. He kicked off his shoes.

It was extraordinary! Everyone was enjoying it:

pleased to be able to have a few words. As speaker after speaker got up, they were rewarded with roars of approval.

One after the other: Audrey had not seen half of them before, they got up, naming their heart's desire, then saying that they might as well not have bothered wanting whatever it was, in the first place, if their feet weren't dry. Some of them were making it up, of course.

Then Petersen got up. He looked yellow in the candle-light. 'After a day's pickings,' he said.

They waited.

'Like what I've here.' He held up his flask. For a moment it looked as if he was stuck for words. Then he said: 'Bits of things. The likes of which you wouldn't understand. If I've got all them bits of things ...'

'Yes?' a voice said encouragingly.

'And I ain't got dry feet, then I ain't got nothing!'

Everyone roared and stamped. Bessie Ottershaw had disappeared.

Unable to stand the heat, desperate to escape from the pain and absurdity of the gathering; like a prisoner slipping his bonds, the Major, doing it as privately as he could, took off his socks.

'Oh, Dad!' said Audrey, taking his hand.

~

As Petersen had been talking the street door had opened. A tall distinguished gentleman with the brief-case was being pointed and guided and pushed to the table where the Major now sat removing his socks. This was none other than Mr Parker, who had been directed to Fellini's by Mrs Oliphant.

Mr Fellini, who had joined the top table and now sat
with them, had noticed the Major's action and was
smiling with approval. He stood up and beckoned to
Alberto.

The stranger, holding a handkerchief to his nose, and
quite unprepared for the possibility of the Major's presence in such a foul place, said: 'I have business with Mr
Weismann. Is he here?'

'A moment please. Alberto! You take Major
Oliphanti's socks.'

Alberto tottered, then rallied and said, 'I don't take
no socks!'

'Alberto!'

'But everybody then starts!'

'Put down those dishes and take the socks. Don't you
want no job?'

'I got a job.'

'Not if you don't take no socks.'

'It's not worth a fuss, Mr Fellini,' said Audrey quietly.
Several people were now listening.

Mr Parker said: 'Good Lord, Henry, is that you?'

~

Suddenly the party broke up. The sunlight dazzled their
eyes as they gathered round the government car, which
was now hemmed in by the crowd.

Bernie was in conversation with Mr Parker. Mary was
there also, and kissed Audrey fondly, bidding her goodbye.

Audrey hugged her father, overwhelmed, grateful
that he had come; it had been for her sake; she knew
that.

'It wasn't so bad, after all, was it, Dad? And I thought you were marvellous! And thanks again.'

'Nothing to thank,' he said, managing a smile.

'And the wellies. I'll see to it!'

'I know you will,' he said. 'And I'm proud of you.'

'Oh, Dad!'

Oliver clasped his father's hand for an instant just as someone appeared to butt George Inkpin in the back.

'Well, we made it, Olly!' Audrey smiled.

Mr Parker unlocked the briefcase from his wrist and was handing the contents to Bernie. It was a list of known routes of government cars throughout the country and the whereabouts of government officials in case of trouble. 'I'm glad I managed to get to you in time,' he said.

'So, who says there'll be trouble?' asked Bernie.

'Just in case,' said Mr Parker, shaking hands.

The Major turned away, and in that instant, Parker, who did not wish to be embarrassed by a conversation, saw his opportunity, and edged quickly towards the government car.

He called back, 'Goodbye, Henry!'

The Major looked about him wildly. Audrey pressed his hand. He was without his socks, without his dignity; his wretchedness complete. He blinked, as he tried to focus on Mr Parker, his eyes still unaccustomed to the bright light.

'I never expected it,' he muttered, 'never thought Nosey ...'

'Well, it's the day the government car often goes through, after all,' Audrey said. ''Bye again.'

Now Bernie started up the old Bentley and slowly

moved off towards the Ossington Road out of town, to stop first at his house to collect Cherry. A moment later, the government car left also. The crowd became quiet and turned away.

~

'Well, this is it!' said Bernie softly, as they started off again with Cherry on board.

They took the road which avoided Ossington town.

Oliver was operating W.H.I.F.F. He called out, 'Lower scooper!'

'Scooper lowered,' said Bernie, reducing speed.

Audrey stroked Cherry's head and was already making plans for their return. Perhaps she could get her parents to have tea at the Inkpins, and then actually meet Mrs Crabbe and Mr and Mrs Perkins?

How could Audrey have known; or Oliver, or Bernie, or indeed any of the people who were now far behind: the Major, Mrs Oliphant, the Inkpins, even Petersen, who had stood on Ossington tip, from which he had watched the shadowy hills long after they had left, unmindful of the flies on his neck; how could any of them have known that there would be no return the following week, or the one after that?

20

On the Road

Two hours after passing Ossington, Bernie had pulled in to read the map, and now, in the distance, they could hear the sound of a vehicle approaching the main road.

'It's the oddest car I've ever seen!' said Oliver, as it hammered up the slope, steam coming out of a funnel.

They waved, but when the driver saw them, he bent down; frantically shovelled in what appeared to be coal, and then with a roar of escaping steam and a sudden belching of smoke, the car moved off at a fair speed in the direction they would be taking.

'It's a steam car,' said Bernie. 'I haven't seen one since the fossil fuel riots put an end to that sort of thing.'

'Did you see how scared he looked, when he saw us? He probably thought we were a government car,' said Oliver.

'Shall we say hello to him and put his mind at rest?' Audrey suggested.

But as they approached, the steam car slowed down and the driver pulled a lever above his head. A cloud of filthy black smoke poured over the Bentley and Bernie slammed on the brakes. By the time they had cleaned the windscreen, the steam car had disappeared. Once or twice from the distance they could hear a series of puffs as it ascended a hill.

'This delay is just what we need,' protested Bernie ... 'And we're due at the Red Lion by nightfall!'

After booking in, they had quickly found the Avon Lady's house following Mavis' directions. Bernie had invited the Avon Lady, Sarah Hopkins, to dinner, and they now sat in the dining room at the back of the inn.

'We've only cold food,' said the landlord.

'Naturally,' replied Bernie. 'My car and trailer will be safe in the car park? I've a government pennant and there's a dog in there, guarding our property.'

'You've left some space for air?' the Avon Lady asked.

'In this heat? I certainly have!'

'We've rabbit pie, pork pie, a selection of cheeses, and rhubarb wine,' the landlord informed them, after reassuring Bernie.

'It sounds absolutely marvellous,' said the Avon Lady, who was short with a creased neck and a jolly smile.

'I'll tell you how we intend going about it,' said Bernie after they had made their choice from the menu. 'The idea,' he said, 'is that we call on Miss Longbotham's Ladies, but only those who live in the larger towns and cities: Ladies like you, in fact. And we're appointing you as collector for this area, which means that you will contact as many Ladies in nearby towns and villages as you are able to reach.'

'Oh, wonderful!' she replied.

'May I ask what size shoe you take?' he added immediately.

'Size five. But you mustn't!'

'I insist '

'You lovely man!'

'But only after a thousand old pairs have been collected,' Audrey reminded her uncle.

'What a challenge!' said the Avon Lady.

'Miss Longbotham has suggested the Ladies collect
the wellies in prams,' said Bernie.

'We'll love it: what then?' she asked.

'I will visit the Town Clerk, who I'm sure will arrange
for the wellies to be picked up and put somewhere safe
for collection by our lorries when it is possible to do so.'

'There'll be no holding us Ladies back, you know,'
she said. 'We're all out of practice; quite wretched
really!'

After Sarah Hopkins had left, and they were going to
their rooms, Audrey said: 'She seems very enthusiastic.
I hope they are all like that.'

Her room overlooked a small courtyard. Down below, gleaming in the lamplight from the kitchen, was
the steam car.

Audrey knocked softly on Bernie's door. After looking up and down the corridor, she whispered: 'It's the
steam car. I can see it from my window.'

~

'Nice little town you have here,' said the same man,
sitting himself down to breakfast.

Bernie moved his head a little, as much as to say,

'Perhaps!'

'Name's Jackson; friends call me Spindly. Live near the Forest of Dean. Small coal mines; uncle works in one. I'm in spreads.'

'What sort of spreads?' asked Bernie.

'Savoury spreads: liver, meat extracts, many more. Sweet spreads, greengage, plum jam; an endless variety. In the trade we call them spreads,' the tall man said wiping his mouth with his napkin. 'Lots of orders. Also curry pastes. Load up; deliver; come back again on a different route, and get more orders. Plenty of coal where I live; fine for cooking and travel.'

'But it's illegal,' Bernie said.

The man winked. After a while he spoke again. 'Fusion power is just around the corner. Time for spreads, for selling, for business, is right now, before the rush starts. There's movement, sir,' added the tall man, in spite of Bernie's continuing silence. 'There's more power in the mornings. It's beginning to happen, I assure you. I'm an early bird. I always have been; and I'm in there first, you see, calling at shops. Why, they'd give me orders for anything! It brings back the old times. But I keep clear of Gloucester; too many police.'

'How do you manage to do it?'

'It's a gift,' said Mr Jackson. 'I mean, travel.' There was a slight pause. 'I have a vehicle,' he said. 'She's a real beauty; a steam car. I call her Friend of Mother Earth. She has a name plate to that effect. Stops people feeling too violent.'

'Don't you ever get stopped?' smiled Bernie. 'In any case, I thought most of them were destroyed in the fossil fuel riots.'

'They are rarities, yes, they are rarities,' the other replied. 'And I keep off the routes used by government cars. I'd thought of calling her Early Bird, instead, after myself. What d'you think?' he asked.

'It's up to you,' said Bernie, helping himself to more cold sausage. 'I have no feelings one way or the other.'

'It would be more truthful,' said Audrey.

'Yesterday we tried to pass you,' said Bernie, adding, as the tall man turned pale, 'but do not be alarmed, Mr Jackson, I am not an official. Sure, I've got a permit and a pennant on my Bentley. What we're doing,' he said, changing his mind, as Audrey kicked his leg 'is ... er, confidential, really.'

'Interesting line, eh?' said Mr Jackson, now reassured.

'Yes, it is, isn't it, Olly? Uncle? But we are forbidden to speak,' Audrey said.

'I'm staying here today, before moving on. If you think I can be of any help to you, here's my card.'

~

'I don't like it,' Audrey said, biting her lip. 'I mean the fact that Mr Jackson is travelling around. There must be others doing the same thing. Perhaps one day soon, another wellington manufacturer will have the same ideas?'

'My father said that Dunlops of Liverpool were recycling wellies long before the Collapse,' Oliver reminded them.

'Yes, but they never got down as far south as this. There are still millions of wellies out there!' said Bernie.

'So, then, we've got to hurry it up,' Audrey replied.

Bernie shrugged. 'We can't; I only wish we could. It takes several days to fill up with liquid gas, you know that, even with S.T.I.N.K.'s help.'

'All the same,' said Audrey,' I think we should start more welly dumps without delay. Now that we're miles from home, we should do just that and not return so soon: travelling back again is only a waste of time. If I write to my parents, would that be all right? And you, Olly, what about you?'

'As far as my parents are concerned, anything which helps with wellies ...' he grinned.

Bernie said: 'I could give the letter to the next government car we see. I'll address it to Parker; he'll see that Henry gets it.'

~

Later, downstairs, Audrey saw Mr Jackson. On an impulse, tapping the letter thoughtfully on her wrist, she said: 'Do you ever go to Ossington?'

'It's funny you should say that,' he said, glancing at her hand.

'It's in the opposite direction to the one you're taking,' she reminded him.

'Round trips,' he said.

'What about Newtown; do you know that?'

'Do I know it!'

'You'd deliver a letter?'

'With pleasure,' he said.

~

They were working the tip. Gulls and crows crowded over the recently dumped rubbish. Audrey was thinking:

Dad would have hated this, and I'm beginning to hate it, too. She looked at Oliver, as he stumbled about.

'Using S.N.I.F.F. is horrible, really, in spite of S.T.I.N.K.,' she said.

'It's cool,' Oliver grinned, wiping his face, 'when you think about the travelling.'

But Bernie was clearly agitated, too. 'This is too new,' he muttered. 'We need to look for older rubbish, and at this rate,' he added grimly, 'we'll need more than just a few days extra, that's for sure! What we need is an idea.'

'Not another one!' said Audrey, with some misgiving.

~

Finding a place where the wellingtons would be stored was easier.

'You're the Town Clerk, I believe? I want a welly site. Oliphants Footwear.' Then Bernie told him everything.

'And these Avon Ladies will do it for nothing?'

'They get a pair of new wellies for a thousand old pairs.'

'What's in it for me?' asked the Town Clerk.

'A new pair for you, too, and straight away. What size do you take?'

'Elevens. You can have a site by the old gas works. No trouble. Glad to help out,' said the Town Clerk.

'Well done, Uncle !' breathed Audrey.

'That's not all,' said Bernie, as Audrey and Oliver listened, perplexed. 'I want something else. I want permission to install a device on your town rubbish tip. It will be kept locked at all times and only I and drivers of government cars will have a key to it.'

21

The Fantastic P.O.N.G.

'I have a new idea,' explained Bernie as they sat down to supper.

'If you mean an invention, then haven't we got enough?' sighed Audrey.

'We're weighed down with equipment, as it is,' Oliver said.

'Exactly!' Bernie replied. 'And having a load of new wellies doesn't help. But listen: this won't add to it.' He paused. 'Believe me, S.M.E.L.L. is a wonderful thing. And where would we be without W.H.I.F.F.?'

'Where, indeed?' said Oliver, glancing across at Audrey.

'S.N.I.F.F. of course, is important too.'

'We don't doubt it, Uncle, but really, why more inventions?'

'It's not a new invention, I promise. Let me explain: with S.T.I.N.K. we can now see the really good places inside. That speeds up S.N.I.F.F.'s work.'

'We all know that,' said Oliver.

'But if, because we can now see exactly where to do it, we made a hole into the tip and placed S.M.E.L.L. over it ...'

'You mean we're going to do away with S.N.I.F.F.?' Audrey gasped. 'And after all the trouble we've had, and Dad getting upset and everything?'

'I'd have to make a few changes to S.M.E.L.L. Cement it in position; keep it locked, so that only we and Parker's people can use it. Meanwhile we go on welly-ing. That's what you wanted, isn't it?'

'It will need power, won't it?' Oliver asked.

'It's on for two hours a day. I can fix that,' replied Bernie.

'So then, having come all this way, we now stay in one place?' Audrey was near to tears.

'No, there would be S.M.E.L.L.s everywhere; on most of the rubbish tips,' Bernie said.

'All the effort, Uncle, inventing S.N.I.F.F. and S.T.I.N.K. Couldn't you have thought of it before?'

'Angel, how could I have afforded it? Parker is making hundreds of them; all they have to do is fix them in position on the tips, instead of carrying them in the government cars. They will have to stop making S.N.I.F.F.s, of course.'

'Then we can go from tip to tip, from S.M.E.L.L. to S.M.E.L.L., just filling up?' she said, beginning to understand.

'Yes, and meet all those Avon Ladies,' Bernie said.

Audrey smiled, and said in a low voice: 'I'm sorry I doubted you.'

~

'In a way I'll be sorry to say goodbye to all those other inventions,' Audrey remarked.

'We'll still have W.H.I.F.F., I suppose?' asked Oliver, who enjoyed working the scooper.

'And the others, too,' Bernie assured them. 'We may need them, you see, if the P.O.N.G. we planned to use had been emptied by a government car.'

'Oh for goodness sake, dear Uncle, what on earth is that?' asked Audrey, beating her head.

'What self-respecting person would go around talking about fixed smells?' he replied. 'P.O.N.G. stands for Privately Owned Natural Gas.'

'Why not?' smiled Audrey.

'Now, the sooner we can get on with it, the better; the moors, the mountains: I can't wait! And wellies all over the place.'

'Thousands of them,' said Oliver.

'I want you to stay with Sarah Hopkins, the Avon Lady, for a few days until I get back. I'm going to see Parker; his headquarters are just twenty-five miles from here.'

~

'It's good news,' said Bernie.

'It's all seen to?' Oliver smiled.

'I've no doubt that already ten or more P.O.N.G.s are on the way to tips on our main route. It's been given top priority. Now, at last, we can start, in earnest.'

~

One day, they passed an old-looking ambulance which had drawn into the roadside, its huge gas bag lying limply over the roof. As Bernie stopped to give what assistance he could, an elderly man scrambled away from him, up the roadside bank, wheezing loudly.

'Are you ...' he puffed, 'a government man?'

'Certainly not,' smiled Bernie. 'What's the matter?'

'Got a hole in me gas bag.'

'I'll tow you into the next town,' said Bernie.' I've no doubt you can get gas there. Do you have a casualty on board?'

'D'you like cold cooked chicken, well, as cold as can be expected; pickled onions, smoked sausage, and home made cakes 'n things? Can't keep the icing right in this weather; tends to hang over the edges ...' So saying, he opened the back door, on the inside of which was painted 'Ronnie's Retail'.

'Isn't it risky pretending to be an ambulance?' Bernie asked.

'I've always lived dangerously,' said the man. 'It's in my nature. Help yourself to a little of what you fancy, for your kindness.'

'We won't have the chicken, thank you,' said Audrey, fearing for their health and safety.

Later Bernie said: 'We're just in time, you know, with your father's wellies. People are beginning to move around, that's for sure; and you were right to be worried.'

And once, as they were crossing the Pennines, they were approached by another steam car, which let off a cloud of steam and passed them at speed.

They saw one or two government cars; some emergency vehicles; and horses and carts bringing in produce off the fields.

Most of the time they were alone. Wherever they stopped they heard only bird song and the lowing of cattle; maybe the sound of church bells. The mists rose in the heat of each day, and settled in the valleys and low-lying fields, at night.

Once as they were descending a hill after dark, below them and as far as they could see beyond the towns and cities on the horizon, the lights came on.

Bernie stopped. It all lasted for no more than two minutes.

Oliver was leaping about on the road, jabbing his finger at the sky, shouting: 'Look at it; look at it!'

But Audrey could not speak. She was trembling with surprise, with happiness; thinking of her parents ... so many feelings!

Bernie said quietly: 'They're testing, probably. Putting fusion power into the grid. It won't be long now!'

~

Everywhere they met with kindness and enthusiasm from the Avon Ladies, and with interest from the Town Clerks.

They went from P.O.N.G. to P.O.N.G., from county to county, forever moving, it seemed; sometimes using W.H.I.F.F.

Their wellington stocks were now nearly finished.

'We've just one pair left; that's one more Town Clerk, then we'll have to turn around for home,' said Bernie.

'It's been fantastic!' said Audrey. 'Dad will be over the moon.'

On their way back they travelled the road where they had met Mr Jackson. But they never saw him or his steam car again.

Mr Jackson had read Audrey's letter, and finding that it contained no secrets, only a reassurance to her parents that they would be home as soon as possible, although much later than planned, had thrown it in amongst the coal before setting off towards the Forest of Dean.

22

Mission Complete

In spite of the S.L.A.P.s in his wellies, the Major's feet were feeling sweaty. He knew P.A.L.S. was a better name for them; Bernie was right, of course. He hated the clamminess; and all that went with it: the huge banks of mist; the swollen streams; the roar of the winds and the suddenness of their stopping; the following sound of sweet bird song from the trees and tall grasses, as if nothing had happened to the weather. He longed for the old times. To add to the general wretchedness, Priscilla was moping, worried about Audrey. He was, too.

It was now long after the date when they should have returned, and he was keeping increasingly to himself. He often stood by Sir Edwin, wishing he too was stone. He avoided talking to people, as much as he could.

He had met Mrs Crabbe in the High Street. He couldn't avoid her.

'The poor Inkpins!' she said, 'They're both beside themselves with worry about Oliver. And there's

Audrey ...' she said, laying a hand upon his arm.

He walked unsteadily to Oliphants Footwear. He gazed at the benches and the covered-over machinery.

For the sake of money he had allowed his daughter to go on a journey which was full of danger. Parker had mentioned the possibility of trouble; at the time he had pretended not to hear him warning Bernie, so determined was he to make a fortune with recycling his wretched wellingtons!

He cursed the machines and the ghosts of trimmers past: 'I would give all of this! All of this,' he cried out, 'to know that she is safe.'

He went to the Inkpins. 'No doubt they'll be back soon,' he said. Mrs Inkpin had taken one look at his face, which was a good deal thinner these days and had assured him in a whisper that she thought so, too, and she had then asked him to stop for a bit of meat stew with her and George. He watched, fascinated, as the bits of carrots kept on sinking and reappearing while she ladled it.

On his way home, there was Bessie Ottershaw! She actually smiled. It did not last long; it was more like a twitch, but it was filled magically, none the less, with pity for him.

Mrs Crabbe had shown the same kindness. Now the Ottershaw woman ... it was unbelievable! He was filled with shame; with an overwhelming gratitude for her kindness. Then she walked by, her nostrils inflated, as if to catch the wind, ending the possibility of a proper greeting.

Mr Fellini too, saw him, as he walked by. He called out: 'You heard from Bernie?'

The Major gazed about uncertainly. At one point it looked as if he was about to speak. Instead he pulled out a handkerchief and mopped his face and neck.

Mr Fellini put his arm around the Major's shoulder, saying: 'I've no doubt ...'

'Absolutely,' replied the Major, not wishing to discuss the possible meaning of their disappearance ... A broken bridge perhaps; and anything could have happened. A cloud of gnats circled over them. Then the Major found himself wandering into the café, overwhelmed again with gratitude at people's kindness; their concern not just for Audrey, but for him.

Now, shaking with confusion as he discovered his affection for those whom he had despised so long, he called out: 'What d'you have, Alberto?'

'Spaghetti al burro, spaghetti napolitana, spaghetti with meat balls. You name it, we got it!'

'My socks, Alberto!'

'I don't take no socks.'

'Alberto, for me, this once,' said the Major, struggling to remove them. 'It is important, you understand. You must believe me!'

Mr Fellini said: 'Alberto don't take no socks, Major.'

'He doesn't?' said the Major, not really caring too much about it; close to tears.

'We just had a visit from the Environmental Health Officer,' said Mr Fellini, 'and we've been given a warning.'

~

On his return he comforted Priscilla. 'I am sure every-thing is all right,' he said, 'and that we'll see them again soon.'

Strangely now, although he could not account for it, he believed this.

Weeks had now passed.

In the meantime he had returned to the café to assure Mr Fellini that he would help next time an official called.

~

It was Alberto who had come to the house to inform the Major that Mr Fellini was in trouble.

'Don't worry,' said the Major, 'I'll come over right away and fix it.'

'I also fix it,' said Alberto mysteriously.

At Fellini's, the Major asked: 'How is it that your vehicle is equipped with a gas bag? I thought it was only the police and emergency services.'

'Since last week it's also the Environmental Health Officers,' said the official grimly, 'and I am investigating the drying of socks where food is being cooked and served in the kitchen.'

'I shall refer the whole matter to Parker,' said the Major.

'Well, I've never heard of him,' said the official.

He came back a moment later, licking his lips with anger.

'Someone's punctured my gas bag!'

'So, then why don't you stay for spaghetti?' asked Mr Fellini.

'You'll hear from me again, believe me,' spluttered the official, ignoring the offer.

The Major wrote a long letter to Parker. He mentioned the suffering of people; he wrote a few words
about dry feet. Dryness! It was dryness of the feet which
comforted mankind, womankind, Grannies, Grandpas,
small people, that sort of thing. The government, the
rulers, the social workers, police, judges; the Fanshaws
of the world, should all give certificates to people connected with dry feet.

Mrs Oliphant read the letter and suggested one or
two improvements.

He then gave it to the driver of the first government
car he was able to flag down, with instructions that was
it was to be sent to Mr Parker with the least delay.

~

Parker himself called. He agreed that the Major had
made an important point; that dry feet could do won-
ders for the national morale and then produced a licence
for Mr Fellini to continue with his Dry Socks Facility, as
it was referred to, as long as it was not handled with the
food.

'But all this,' Parker had then said, 'is bye-the-bye. I
mean we don't aim to get involved with people like
Fellini, doing this with his socks, just as in the same way
we didn't want to get involved with your brother-in-
law's frog-scooper.'

'Then why ..?'

'It's a personal favour, Henry. Mind you, we agree
absolutely with the principles. The far more important
thing we can do and must do fast, in view of this wet
feet business ...' he paused. 'You know, Henry, you
really should write a book about it one day.'

'You think so?'

'I do: what would you call it?' asked Mr Parker.

'The Thing To Do,' said the Major without hesitation.

'What thing, Henry?' asked Parker, somewhat taken aback.

'Oh nothing, really.'

'Anyway, to continue,' Parker said, 'it's this: you must get your lorries on the road without delay. I've brought pennants with me and the necessary documents; also I've a list of the P.O.N.G.s agreed with Mr Weismann. Your lorries will take their fuel from the P.O.N.G.s, of course.'

'I beg your pardon?' asked the Major.

Mr Parker told him again. Then he told him once more, although the Major seemed to keep on missing bits of it.

'They're safe?'

'Of course they are!'

'Due here? Perhaps tomorrow?'

'I told you, Henry! Of course you'll have a permit to manufacture.'

He was shaking. 'I never. Well, I never!' Then weakly he asked: 'What are P.O.N.G.s?'

~

The power was on for longer now. Three hours a day; sometimes four. The lorries rolled in with old wellies, some of which had notes pinned on them. One read: 'With love from the Avon Ladies of Macclesfield'; another: 'No to Dry Skin; Yes to Dry Feet, from the Avon Ladies of Luton.' And so on. The lorries rolled out again with new ones.

Each delivery included free wellies for the Avon Ladies and their families, with a letter of thanks from the Major and one from Mavis, who had by this time been invited to join the Avon Head Office, if she could find the means of getting there.

The King's Birthday Honours List, as shown on morning television, included both Bernie and the Major, both of whom were awarded the O.B.E.; Bernie for providing emergency fuel cover for Government vehicles and for his contribution to the environment: using methane gas which would otherwise leak and further damage the atmosphere, and the Major for his contribution to the national morale by supplying recycled wellingtons and at a price which everyone could afford, rather than making an easy fortune out of people's misery.

Meanwhile the choppers shook and roared; the shakers shook the bits of wellies through sieves; the hot plastic surged through the presses; all of it to George's delight!

Most nights Bernie had dinner with the family, to Mary's great satisfaction, although sometimes he would be away for several days helping Parker's people if they were having problems with a P.O.N.G. The Major sometimes went with him; Audrey and Oliver too, if it was during their holidays.

The Major and Bernie were good friends; united in purpose.

They had never been before! It happened this way:

It was before the first load of wellies had been sent out, and whilst the thought amongst the people of Newtown and Ossington and the surrounding villages of having dry feet burned into them like a fever.

Early one morning the Major called his workers to-gether in the factory and gave them each a pair of wellies. Bessie, who had been appointed Head Trim-mer, could not stop her teeth from chattering. She kept on saying, 'Well, I never!'

He then asked Bernie to help him. They gave wellies to the poor and needy in Newtown and then went in the Bentley to Ossington and did the same.

They called on the vicar; Mr Hood the pig farmer, at Bernie's request; then at Mr Petersen's house of carpet and tin.

'I don't understand you,' Bernie had said. 'What's got into you?'

The Major was sweating; he was jubilant. He said: 'Nothing much, except that when I thought I would never see Audrey ... any of you, again; and I had not heard from you!'

'It was Spindly Jackson,' said Bernie.

'People I'd not spoken to; hardly knew them. Mrs Crabbe. Been beastly to some of them. Came up to me. Asked: "Have you heard?" Very moving,' said the Major.

By the afternoon they had given away over five hun-dred pairs.

'You'd better go easy now, Henry. You're running a business, after all,' warned Bernie.

'Every pair of wellingtons ... like chains slipping from me: feel like a new man, Bernie!'

'I understand,' Bernie replied softly, 'but now it's time to go home.'

'Come and have dinner with us,' the Major said.

'Hello, what's this?' said Bernie later as they approached the Major's house. A dozen or so people were on the doorstep.

Audrey greeted them: 'There's more inside, Dad.'

'They wish to thank you, dear,' said Mrs Oliphant.

'Come in,' said the Major to those on the steps. 'Mary! Go to the cellar and bring up the port. All of it.'

Bernie was smiling happily, talking to Priscilla, saying: 'He could have made a fortune with that lot of wellies!'

The Major overheard them and said, surveying the people crowding into the sitting room and in the corridors: 'This is my fortune!'

Bessie Ottershaw had come in and was moving towards the Major. There were candles everywhere, of course. A voice like Petersen's was heard to say: 'You ain't got nothing!'

Bessie came up to the Major, put her arms round his neck and kissed him, and then to everyone's delight and to Audrey's especially, he did the same to Bessie.

The lights came on.

Everyone stopped talking. They stayed still. Mrs Oliphant was standing next to Audrey. Oliver and George were close by. Mavis Longbotham, who had simply called in having heard there was a party, was being shown how a Hot Box worked, by Mr Fellini. They now stood motionless.

Then, after a few seconds, the power had gone off again, as they knew it would.

The Major broke the silence: 'It won't be long, now. A few months, Parker said. Make wellies all day long, not just a few hours. Night-shifts, too.'

'And let's get it right, this time. All of us: the manu-facturers, the people who want the things they make. Get it right with the packaging, the waste, the rivers, the air,' Bernie said.

'Also remember: wellies not everything,' said the Major, as his voice was drowned once again by the rising chatter and laughter.

Bernie and the Major had glanced at each other, then had suddenly embraced, slapping each other on the back, calling each other by name, as if they had not met for years, as indeed, in a sense, they had not.

As the party was by now altogether rowdy, no one took the slightest notice, except Audrey and her mother, who, on seeing this, gently embraced too.

Audrey said: 'Everything's all right now, isn't it?'

~

Mr Petersen died in the winter, but not before the Major to his great credit, for it was not a pleasant thing to do, had taken a swig from the flask. He had done so, a month previously, to his relief, for such a chance to show him his respect in this way, had now ended for-ever.

Also by John Wood

IN A SECRET PLACE

It was no ordinary trip to the woods for Alice, Yanina, Paul and Benjamin. Yet they never expected to come upon Lord Augustus!

It was an adventure that coloured their lives. And Alice, at least, was determined to return to that secret place, to feel again the magic and half-dream.   £3.99

Shortlisted for the Irish Book Awards 1987.

CHARLIE AND THE STINKING RAGBAGS

Charlie Smith's world is a world full of smells!

The musty smell of the derelict car where his friend Sid the duck usually lives; the smell of meat roasting, although he almost never gets to taste any; the different smells of pond water and river water; and of his Grandma's Lavender Water. But the most fascinating smell of all is the smell of the Stinking Ragbags — the down and outs who gather in the town to beg at Christmas. And it is this particular smell which leads Charlie by the nose into all sorts of trouble ... £3.99

TROUBLE AT MRS PORTWINE'S

Nominated for the Carnegie Medal. Shortlisted for the Irish Book Awards

Ferdie and Geordie live in a shed. Things might be better if their father didn't have such a passion for sausages ... For one thing, they wouldn't have to steal Mrs Portwine's famous sausages and, in return, spend their nights secretly washing dishes in her café — with unexpected consequences when they become entangled in Samantha's selfish schemes ...   £6.95 hardback / £3.99 paperback.

'Imaginative and extremely well-written, it paints in people and places vividly ... a lively and unusual tale.' Irish Times

Available from your bookseller or from
WOLFHOUND PRESS
68 Mountjoy Square, Dublin 1
Tel 01 874 0354. Fax 01 872 0207
Call or write for our catalogue.

To my grandchildren

My thanks to Bob Harrington of Dunlop Footwear Ltd, Liverpool, who so kindly showed me round the wellington factory and explained everything.

W.H.I.F.F.!